MOST PECULIAR WAYS

MOST PECULIAR WAYS

TREY LETCHER

ISBN-13: 978-1-7367878-4-7 (*Paperback*)

For "Dump"

TABLE OF CONTENTS

MOST PECULIAR WAYS 1

TEENAGE LOVE 59

INTRODUCING EMILY 93

THE SANDSTONE CROSS 143

MOST PECULIAR
WAYS

I GOTTA GET a hold of his folks," Frankie heard his father whisper. "Get his body back to North Carolina."

Little Frankie hadn't witnessed his friend go down. He was standing at his usual spot by the bally stage watching his father work the crowd when he heard the commotion. He'd just started toward the tent when Pokey came running out and hooked him under the arm. "It's bad, Frankie," he said, dragging him away. "You...you don't wanna see this, little man." His voice sounded funny.

Pokey left Frankie sitting alone at a picnic table near their end of the midway, then hurried back to the scene. Frankie watched as folks spilled out of the tent and into the lamplight, hands over their mouths, heads shaking. Soon, vehicles came with flashing red lights. He watched his father, Frank Jameson Jr., speaking with a police officer, his hands going from his hips to the top of his head and back to his hips. Then someone pushed a table with wheels into the tent. When it came out a good while later, something large and white and motionless lay upon it.

"Bad knee's actin' up on me, boss," Frankie remembered Jarvis telling his father earlier that day.

"Have Lois rub it down" had been his father's reply. "Get

ya some willow bark to chew on. We come all this way, damned if I ain't gonna get mine from these backwoods chumps."

After the ambulance had driven off, Pokey Harpeth, his twin Jeb, and Little Lois McGhee walked around the set dazed, wiping tears from their faces and sharing hugs. Jameson, who had joined his son at the picnic table, sat on the tabletop hunched over with his dusty boots on the bench where Frankie sat. "Hell, I reckon I'm gonna need all the strength I can find...get us through this," Jameson said. He removed a bottle from the inside pocket of his red rhinestone-encrusted western jacket and took a long pull. He noticed his son staring up at him, his bottom lip quivering. Jameson flapped his own lips together mockingly. "What, boy? You got somethin' to say?"

Frankie lowered his head and fixed his gaze on his father's cowboy boots. He flinched when his father yelled, "Get the hell outta here, you damn vultures." The few lingering bystanders stood balking, their jaws slack, eyes wide with insult. When they made no move to leave, Frank Jameson stood on the bench and hurled the bottle in their vicinity. The amber glass shattered, giving their trouser legs a good dose of Dr. Frank's Strength and Stamina Serum.

• • •

They had traveled sixty miles in silence, the distress obvious on Jameson's mustached face. Frankie held back the tears; crying would only set his father off. A road sign indicated they had crossed the Myer County line. Jameson followed the main road that led into the small Southern Appalachian town of Olivia. "Preston's printshop's here," Jameson said at last.

"'Member? Reach back there and gather up a dozen or so of them posters."

The caravan, which transported the medicine show all over the southeastern states, included a 1930s model GMC sleeper cab, which Jameson's father, Frank Jameson Sr., had purchased at an auction. Once the asset of a failed storage and moving company, the old branding along the trailer it pulled was quickly overlaid with a vibrant new banner promoting "DR. FRANK'S PATENT MEDICINE AND ENTERTAINMENT COMPANY." The rest of the team trailed Jameson and his son in a rusted-out Dodge humpback delivery truck that took every ounce of the twins' mechanical ingenuity to keep running.

Frankie turned and got on his knees. He rummaged through the sleeper compartment, returning with a small stack of posters he began neatening on his lap. They'd been printed months earlier. Thrifty Frank had the foresight to leave plenty of white space at the bottom to allow for dates, times, and locations of upcoming shows to be overprinted. Unfortunately, he'd not foreseen his most lucrative human attraction collapsing in a lifeless heap under the weight of the massive hay bale.

The first post-Jarvis show took place at a county fair near the Tennessee-Georgia border. The secrecy surrounding his father's new hire—a grisly looking elderly man named Samuel—had piqued Frankie's youthful curiosity. That night, as his father commanded the bally stage, Frankie snuck over to the tent where the mysterious Samuel was performing his bit. The cardboard sign above the tent's entrance read, "ADULTS ONLY." Frankie poked his head through the flap. On the platform before a small group of men, the wrinkled gray-bearded Sam stood wearing nothing but an open terry cloth robe. His very large private part was exposed and pointing in the direction of the bare light bulb that hung above the stage.

"Eighty-one years old, folks," Jeb announced proudly as he wound his way through the crowd with a raised bottle of Dr. Frank's new Powerful Potency Potion. "Remember what Dr. Frank says, 'No matter what your age, you can be the man she needs you to be!'"

Frankie had helped with the rebranding effort, using long iron tongs to hold each bottle over a pot of boiling water until the old Strength and Stamina labels could be peeled away.

Alas, old Samuel's tenure had lasted but two nights. He absconded from Dr. Frank's Traveling Medicine Show, leaving a hundred bottles of liquid-laced methamphetamine with no viable attraction to market them.

Jameson glanced down at his son, whose short chubby finger was following the arched letters of his dead friend's name, "JARVIS THE GIANT."

"We gotta use 'em anyhow," Jameson told his son coolly. "Ain't had no time to get a new one drawed up. Sooner you forget about Jarvis, the better. Gone is gone, boy."

Frankie shot his father a disapproving glance.

The back of Jameson's hand met the tip of his son's nose with a sound akin to the bite into a cold, crisp pickle. His eyes watered as blood streamed from his nostrils onto the posters in his lap.

"Pinch your nose, goddamnit," his father growled.

While his verbal menaces had been pervasive, Jameson had never laid a hand on his son while Jarvis was alive. Frankie was going to miss his friend.

Jameson turned down Main Street and followed it into

Olivia's downtown business district. He maneuvered the rig into a parking area overlooking the cove's dark waters. He worked the transmission into first gear and cut the engine. The van pulled in behind and sputtered to a stop.

"C'mon," Jameson said, pushing open his creaking door.

Frankie jumped out and followed Jameson, watching his father amble bowlegged toward the van, the wooden soles of his cowboy boots clicking against the wood planks of the lakefront walkway. Little Lois scurried around from behind the van, her lofty, platinum mane bouncing. She gasped for air as if breaking the water's surface after a long immersion.

"Get yer big head back in there," Jameson hollered, quickening his pace.

"Jeb's got gas again, Frank," she explained. "I gotta have some fresh air, or I'm 'fraid I'll lose my breakfast all over the van."

"Back in there!" He aimed a finger at her as his eyes flitted among the few pedestrians strolling leisurely along the waterfront. "We don't give no free previews."

Lois took one last breath and disappeared behind the van. The sound of the back door slamming caused Frankie to jump.

Jameson rapped a knuckle on the driver's side window. Pokey cranked down the glass, releasing flatulent air into his boss's face. Jameson jerked his head back. "Goddamn." He glared at Jeb in the passenger seat. "Somethin' crawl up ya 'n die?"

Jeb shrugged.

"Listen," Frank said to Pokey. "We're goin' down to Preston's shop to get some posters printed up. Frankie and I'll spread 'em around the storefronts. Y'all stay put. If I come back and one of ya's outside the van, I'll shoot ya."

Pokey gave a half-hearted salute.

Inside Preston Printing & Engraving, Frankie immediately glanced toward the back corner of the shop where the colossal letterpress lurked. Built in 1902 by the Chandler & Price Company, the hulking iron machine continued to produce church bulletins, event announcements, and Olivia's single-sheet daily news flyer. Frankie still had the one-of-a-kind print Paul Preston had cranked out for him during their last visit.

Preston greeted father and son with surprise. "Why hello, gentlemen. You doin' a run? I wasn't aware—"

"I know, I know," Jameson said apologetically. "It's been one goddamned thing after another." He gestured toward his son.

Frankie approached the printer carrying the posters in his arms.

"All right then," Preston said, taking one off the top of the stack. "Tell me what you need."

Jameson pointed to the empty space at the bottom and began reciting, "Wednesday and Thursday, first shows startin'—"

"This Wednesday and Thursday?" Preston said, giving Frank a sidelong glance.

"That's right," Jameson replied stiffly.

"Amos's farm again?"

"Same's always," Jameson replied with a hint of annoyance.

"Hmm. Let me see somethin'." Preston returned the poster to Frankie and stepped over to the storefront window. He returned carrying a large advertisement printed on a sturdy paper stock. He handed it to Jameson. Frankie raised his chin and scanned the image, admiring the clean, multicolored design. It had a photographic reproduction of a man wearing a white suit and dark tie. He held a Bible in his left hand, his right hand was held at face level and balled into a threatening fist.

"What's he doin'?" Jameson scoffed. "Gonna punch the Devil in the mouth?"

Preston smiled gamely. "Now, Frank—"

"Tent revival," Jameson began reading aloud. "Gospel and healing service. Evangelist Herman Roscoe joined by miracle boy Little Teddy." Jameson lifted his head and grinned at Frankie. "Hell, we got a little 'un with us too." He returned his focus back to the poster, his grin slowly fading as he continued reading, "August eighteenth through twenty-fourth. Nightly, seven in the p.m. Place, Wildwood Farm off Route nineteen. Everyone welcome."

"Guess I'm not the only one you didn't let know you were coming?" Preston said.

"Since when does Amos rent out to the hallelujah folk?" Jameson asked with a scowl.

"Well, Frank," Preston said, softening his tone, "you knew he lost his wife? This past winter."

Frank shot Preston a surprised glance. "Judith?"

Preston nodded.

Frank stroked his mustache a few times. "I ain't heard that." After a moment, he thrust the poster toward Preston. "What's *that* got to do with *this*?"

"Well..." Preston lowered his head. He moved the toe of his shoe around on the ink-speckled concrete floor. "After a blow like that...forty-five years together... Reckon he just needed somethin' to run to." Preston raised his head toward Jameson. "Sorry, Frank. I guess I don't have to tell *you* that."

Jameson stared at the printer as if waiting for him to make his point.

"Between me and you and the ink cans," Preston continued, "Amos told me he was ready to go the way of his wife. You could see the grief in every crease of his face, poor fella. One night, he thought he might..." Preston paused. "Well, that ain't my story to tell. He ended up cryin' out to God. And, says Amos, the Lord was there for him." Preston glanced at Frankie. "And that's where Amos ran."

Jameson shook the poster at Preston, who took it and raised it to his face. "This boy mentioned here," Preston said. "The boy healer. They say he performs honest-to-God mira—"

"Bullshit," Jameson spat.

Preston continued unaffected. "He was involved in a tent revival up near Greeneville. They were all onstage praying for this one sick child, a girl named Luella. The parents...they'd given up hope. Doctors told 'em nothing left to do but to pray. So they brought her to the tent that night. As Little Teddy prayed over Luella, he began to levitate. Rose three feet off the platform and...just hovered over that baby."

"Beyond bullshit," Jameson said.

"No, no. It happened. I've seen the photograph. And the child? Now healthy as a horse."

"C'mon, boy," Jameson said, yanking Frankie's shirt collar, "'fore we in it up to our necks."

• • •

Frank Jameson leaned into the broad steering wheel as if doing so would somehow hasten their pace. Frankie watched the muscles in his father's quivering jaw, his dark, unblinking eyes fixed and resolute. He spun the wheel with the heel of his left hand and turned onto a long muddy road wet from the overnight rain. They bounced in their seats as the rig lumbered down the slope toward a big red barn and two silo towers.

"I'll be a son of a bitch," Jameson whispered.

Frankie followed his father's gaze to a long white rectangular open-air tent sitting in the middle of the vast green field. Folks were scurrying within and about it, others were trudging up from out of a dense evergreen forest that screened the inlet beyond. Frankie could see tiny camping tents nestled within the trees.

"Well," Jameson said, his mouth growing tight, "there's your damned hallelujah bunch." He breathed heavily through his nose as he struggled to keep to the slippery path.

Frankie felt his heart start to race. His left hand was pressed into the cushioned seat for balance; his right held a white-knuckled grip on the door handle. At last, the truck slid to a stop in front of the barn.

"Stay put," Jameson ordered, then quickly jumped out and slammed the door closed. Frankie watched his father approach a young woman. He said something to her; she pointed. Jameson stomped toward the barn and paused. He leaned down, picked something off the ground, and used it to scrape mud from the soles of his cowboy boots. He tossed the thing back to the ground and disappeared into the dark breezeway.

Frankie anxiously passed the time watching the hallelujah people go about their preparations. Several were off-loading items from a flatbed truck and carrying them onto a massive platform at the front of the tent. Frankie recognized the shape of guitar cases, several speaker boxes similar to those his father used, and some tall white flower arrangements, which were set about the stage.

Frankie caught movement in his periphery. Two young boys emerged from the barn. They paused just outside the breezeway and looked his way. One had an axe resting on his shoulder, cupping a hand over his brow to block the midday sun. The other boy waved, and Frankie waved back. The same boy smiled. Frankie smiled back. Then he heard his father's booming voice.

"What kind of man breaks his word to a friend?"

Both boys quickly glanced behind them. The boy with the axe dropped it and scampered away. The smiling boy held Frankie's gaze a moment longer, then picked up the axe and began walking casually toward the revival tent.

Jameson came stomping out of the barn. He paused to wipe his forehead with his red handkerchief, then came charging toward the truck. He was followed by Amos Tilley, the man who ran Wildwood Farm and lived in the beautiful, tall white house with a green metal roof that Frankie had always admired.

"Answer me that, Amos!" Jameson pressed. He stopped in front of the truck and placed a boot on its front bumper. "Damn it, this is my *business* yer messin' with. You push me out for a bunch of holy rollin' Jesus...*whackos*? I got brand spankin' new window ads comin' hot off the press this very second," he lied.

Amos ambled over with his hands tucked into the pockets of his overalls. He glanced into the cab and gave Frankie a sympathetic smile. Frankie returned a quick, worried nod.

"How long you know me, Amos? Huh? How long you knowed Daddy?"

"I done told ya, Frank. Now that's that. I'm sorry you don't respect my newfound faith, but it's a done deal. All signed for. And I give 'em the possibility of an extension, if the good Lord directs."

"So, it's the missin' ink that's the problem? What happened to two men shakin' hands in agreement on a matter? Now, I know I should've sent word ahead, but—"

"No, Frank. You ain't listenin'. I won't be no part of you hoodwinkin' these poor folks."

"Never thought you'd turn into one of them do-gooders," Jameson admonished. "Anyway..." He cocked his head as he locked eyes with the farmer. "What the hell you think this hallelujah bunch is doin' with their healin' sham?"

Amos shook his head, his expression dismissive.

"And 'poor folks' is right," Jameson continued. "All healin' ain't done by prayer and layin' on hands. For some folks, *I've* got the best solution for what ails 'em. How you servin' your Lord by denyin' folks the medicine they need. I may be an old hell-bound heathen, but that don't sound too awful Christian-like to—"

"Last year," Amos butted in, his tone somber, his expression solemn. "It was early fall. I let a new outfit set up for a three-day run. First night, I come down to have myself a look-see. Make sure it was all square. Fella named Donaldson...fairly big outfit. Had a Ferris wheel, tilt-a-whirl, merry-go-round. Bunch of fun for the youngsters. Looked wholesome enough. There was some entertainment setups too. I moseyed down the midway, enjoyin' my funnel cake, when I seen this raggedy old tent...right at the very end...kind of off to the side and set away from the lights. The banner had this grinnin' Devil-face woman. At first, I was thinkin' it might be some kind of spook show. Funhouse thing. Nobody out there talkin' from the bally stand. Just this one woman near the entrance, dressed in, well, not much. Had her belly exposed. Legs too. Nothin' on but this little see-through number wrapped over bikini bloomers. I look around, and there ain't a child to be seen. I knew right then somethin' stank 'bout the thing. I charged straight into that tent and seen another young woman up on the platform, nothin' on whatsoever, thrustin' them hips this way and that. Some kind of strange chant runnin' through a little speaker sittin' on the edge of the stage."

Frank Jameson took his boot off the bumper and stood tall in his black-and-white thunderbird-embroidered cowboy boots. He hooked his thumbs under the waistband of his trousers. "Now, what's I'm doing got to do with some koochie show, Amos? I peddle my patents. The twins sing some songs. Sure, Lois tells a few racy jokes. Not a one of 'em funny. But that's all there is to it. Who we hurtin', Amos?" He lifted a small cigar from his snap-button shirt pocket and lit it with a silver flip-top lighter. He returned his boot to the bumper, puffing away as Amos continued his recount.

"I seen a line of men off the side of the stage. A one-armed fella standin' guard in front of a heavy drape. Had a metal box sittin' on a stool beside him. I watched him take their money, then hand them something from these little tin containers. Then he'd part the drape and send 'em through. Well, this bein' *my* property, I went right up to this one-armed fella, and, skippin' pleasantries, told him to kindly step aside." Amos's tone turned grave. "Right there, I fell witness to the vilest site I could imagine."

Frank Jameson let out a brazen laugh, a burst of white smoke escaping his mouth. "I don't gotta imagine," he said, shaking his head. "One gal...naked as the day she's born. Had the Devil's grin on her face, did she? Only, by the end of the night, I doubt she was grinning 'neath that mask after twenty or so of them...ah...private performances." Jameson brought the cigar to his face and studied it. "They call her Diablesa in the AB. Amusement business. She's from Tijuana. If what you seen behind that drape turned your tummy, I won't tell you what her specialty was back in her homeland. *Dios mío.*"

"I thank ya not to," Amos said. "I swore right then that this land the Lord has blessed me with will be used for his glorification. Never again for sin to run amok—"

"I thought you reborns was supposed to care 'bout the lowliest among us," Frank said, as if searching for common ground. "Damned if I don't help out the lowliest bunch you ever seen." He stared quietly into the distance for a moment. Finally, he said grudgingly, "Listen, Amos, I've had a bit of a bad turn here lately."

Amos followed his gaze. "I heard about Jarvis, Frank." He shook his head woefully. "Hated to hear it." He faced Frank and confessed, "But I also heard about the old man. Through the grapevine, so to speak."

"Aw, shit now, Amos." Frank rolled his eyes.

"Indecent exposure, Frank?" Amos said incredulously.

"I done lost him too," Frank admitted, his tone turning docile. "He took off with some young gal during our Chattanooga run. Ain't heard boo from him since."

"Well"—Amos dropped his head again and snickered—"I'm sorry 'bout that too."

"Mm-hmm," Frank grunted. "All I got left's two negro albinos and an aging pigmy who's startin' to run her smart-ass mouth a little much for my likin'."

"Listen," Amos said, "it ain't nothin' against you personally. We go back...back to your adolescence. And it wouldn't be Christian of me to turn you away outright."

"'Cept you doin' it."

"Prohibition's long gone, Frank," Amos's tone had turned to one of reason. "Folks ain't gotta come out to a medicine show to get looped on your...*remedies*. They can buy legit. And there's still a weekly run of the rotgut flowin' down from Johnson County. I never understood why you forsook your daddy's sideshow and turned to this—"

"This ain't my daddy's operation. It's *mine*. And I ain't pushin' no giggle juice. Buddy of mine come back from the war, he was missin' that Benzedrine rush they was fed of a mornin'. Who don't wanna feel invincible? I busted my ass to get connected. You don't earn the trust of folks in this particular...*vocation* overnight. Took a hell of a lot of time. You gotta find a doctor credible enough to pass muster with the regulators runnin' yer labels under their damned monocle." Jameson scoffed. "I ain't servin' folks knockout drops, Amos. I'm pickin' 'em up." Jameson glanced back at the dilapidated Dodge van. "Least I was. Not sure how many pints of vigor I'm gonna move with a song and dance bit and a lame joke teller who lost her looks a decade back."

Amos chuckled, earning a quick look of displeasure from his old friend.

"Well, 'fraid you got a point there," Amos said somewhat apologetically. "Folks wanna hear fiddles and harmonies, they got the Opry on the radio. Hell, folks wanna laugh, we got a movie house just fifteen miles up the road. Folks needin' a charge, they don't wait for Dr. Frank to come through town. They pay a visit to their family doctor, then to the local drugstore with a note for fifty tablets. From whatever angle you're lookin', you're workin' a dyin' trade, Frank. A novelty. I'm sorry, but that's just the world we're in now."

"Novelty?" Jameson spat, cutting his eyes at the farmer.

Amos glanced at Frankie again, then blew out a long

breath. "How 'bout this... You're welcome to stay over tonight. Tomorrow night. Long as you need to sort things out. No charge, no nothin'. Got a couple of spare rooms for you and Frankie. I can get the bunkhouse fixed up for the others. Give 'em some steady work here on the farm for a spell..."

Through the open passenger window, Frankie listened hopefully for his father's reply.

Jameson shook his head, then took a drag from the cigar. "We'll stay the night." Jameson nodded toward the wooded area where the revival crew had set up camp. "Down there. You can keep yer charity."

"That's fine, Frank."

"Fine," Jameson quipped. "Now...what 'bout them ad posters Preston's runnin' off? I'm s'posed to pick 'em up in the mornin'. Might be the Christian thing to pay me for my promotional investment?"

Frankie glanced down at the neat stack of posters in his lap.

"All right, Frank," Amos conceded. He removed a roll of bills from the breast pocket of his overalls. "What's Preston chargin' you?"

Jameson spouted an amount.

Thumbing through the bills, Amos said, "I'd also like to offer an invitation to tonight's service. Bring all who wanna come. And there'll be plenty of good food served as well." Amos glanced at Frankie again. "Maybe Frankie'd like to help some of the boys chop wood for the barbeque? Set up tables? That'd give him somethin' to do, keep him busy."

Jameson glanced at Frankie through the windshield.

"No. I got plenty to keep him busy," Jameson said, eyeing the sloppy condition of the road leading through the pasture and into the property's wooded perimeter. He took one last pull from his cigar, then dropped it in the mud and gave it a shallow burial with the pointed toe of his boot. He went to the driver's side door of his truck and hoisted himself onto the footrail. Before climbing into the cab, he turned to Amos and asked, without a trace of humor, "When's supper?"

• • •

Frankie and his father approached the tent at the time Amos had given. Music and singing spilled from under the huge canopy. Outside there were folks setting food and beverage containers on wooden picnic tables and a man working the brick barbeque grill. A tall pile of freshly cut firewood was stacked next to it.

Frank checked his pocket watch and grumbled, "Guess dinner's runnin' late."

Frankie took his father's hand and nodded toward the tent.

"Why the hell not?" Jameson said. "Dinner *and* a show."

Frankie began walking down the center aisle. Jameson yanked his shirt collar and dragged his son backwards. "We're sittin' back here."

He pulled Frankie to the very last row and pushed him into a wooden folding chair. Jameson fell heavily onto the chair beside him. Unlike the medicine show's smaller, claustrophobic enclosure, the revival tent was long and rectangular, its sides open, allowing a soft breeze to flow through. Its canvas was clean and white. In the darkening dusk, the interior was illuminated with hundreds of bulbs dangling from wires strung along the framing poles. The front stage spanned nearly its entire width. A white podium bearing a large simple cross stood center stage.

The tent was only about a quarter full, but it was lively. Frankie had never seen so many happy people. Hands were clapping, heads bobbing, and bodies jerked about as the sound of the instruments resonated through speaker boxes set on tripods at each end of the stage. An elderly lady wearing a long dress, black-rimmed eyeglasses, and a small round hat pounded the piano keys with vigor. Assembled at the back of the stage behind a low dividing wall was a choir of men and women, mostly older whites, but a few as black as Jarvis. They sang with wide smiles fixed on their faces, their hands and heads lifted toward the dangling lights. One man leapt off the stage and began dancing up and down the center aisle like a schoolboy skipping joyfully on a playground. When he'd made it as far as the back row, Frankie recognized him as Evangelist Herman Roscoe on the poster from Mr. Preston's printshop. He danced his way to the front again and climbed the steps at the side of the stage. Just as the song came to an end, Roscoe led them into the next one. His voice rose and fell as he moved close to the microphone stand, then faded when he stepped back to dance and rattle a tambourine over his head.

Frankie spotted a young boy. He thought it must be the miracle-doer, Teddy something. He was with others who stood in front of a row of chairs that lined the dividing wall. Dressed in a white suit identical to Roscoe's, he clapped his hands while marching in place.

When the music ended, Roscoe stepped to the microphone and said breathlessly, "Isn't it a privilege to make a joyful noise for our Lord?"

A chorus of Amens followed.

"Some say, 'Brother Roscoe, all this ruckus you're stirrin'

up when you sing them songs... Why, it's no different than the heathens movin' and shakin' to their jazz or blues records.'"

There came a low rumble of disapproval.

"Well, I don't know 'bout you, but when the Bible tells me to praise your Lord with tambourine and dance, I aim to do it! Especially since I can't play the trumpet and I don't know a lyre from a lamb chop!"

Laughter followed by more amens.

"I can't say what's in the teenagers' heart as they gyrate about to their Devil music, but *I* am singing from a heart filled with thankfulness. I'm singing in the spotlight of the Lord. I'm singing praise with my spirit, folks."

Applause erupted. Frankie saw the boy healer shake his fists in the air, something near a mischievous grin fixed on his cherubic face.

Roscoe wiped his brow with a white towel, then threw it over his shoulder. "Friends...later tonight, after the healing service, we'll come together one more time in praise. And we'll do it with even *more* hope. Even *more* gratitude. *More* conviction. I know it shall be so, because I am confident in my Lord and what he's about to do here tonight. I tell you...he heals today as he did in the days of the New Testament. For our God is the same today as he was then. Hallelujah?

"I want you to turn to the person next to you and say, 'Whatever your ailment, God heals.' Look to them and say, 'Whatever your disease, God heals.' However dire your circumstances may seem to you, God makes all things work for the good."

Frankie glanced at his father. Amongst the jubilant chaos, Jameson sat arms crossed, eyes closed, with his chin resting on his chest.

"I invite you all to break bread with us right outside,"

Roscoe announced. "I'm told we've got plenty, but if we start runnin' low, maybe I'll just ask Jesus to multiply our portions so that every last one of his good people comes back to their seats with a full belly."

• • •

They sat alone at one of the picnic tables outside the revival tent. Frankie watched embarrassed as his father tore chicken flesh and meat from bones with his fingers and teeth, his head held low, his determined eyes trained on the food.

Frankie felt bad for Little Lois and Pokey and Jeb. His father had ordered them to remain back at the campsite with the disparaging suggestion that they gather branches and make a fire to warm the Heinz baked beans they kept stocked in the van. Before heading up to the tent, Frankie had secretly supplied them with half a loaf of Kern's bread from the sleeper compartment of the truck.

"Fill 'er up," Jameson barked, sliding Frankie his empty plate. Then, with his thick black mustache glistening with chicken juice, he said, "Get me a couple of thighs this go-around. I need to get some fat in me. And plenty more of that creamed corn."

As Frankie stood in line to retrieve his father's third help-ing, he spotted Teddy, the boy evangelist. He was standing at a table crowded with baskets of sliced cornbread and alu-minum containers with large ladles set before them. The boy met his gaze. Again, he gave Frankie a smile and a wave. Frankie returned the wave.

When Frankie's turn came at the grill, the big fellow in a stained apron used steel tongs to place a breast of chicken on Frankie's plate.

"Nope. These two, Fred." It was Teddy again. He pointed his finger at a couple of pieces sizzling on the hot grates, the tips of the flames touching the boy's hand.

The man named Fred removed the breast meat from Frankie's plate and replaced it with the two pieces indicated by the boy. "The very last two," he said.

Frankie glanced down at his plate. When he looked up, the boy was gone. At the sides table, Frankie found the creamed corn and spooned a good portion onto the plate, then headed back to the table.

"He hears you," came a whispered voice. Frankie stopped and scanned the crowd of faces. All seemed occupied with food consumption or idle chat. Then he spotted Teddy sitting at a table with Hermon Roscoe and several others. His kind blue eyes held Frankie's gaze for a long moment before he rejoined the conversation with his dinner mates.

Jameson enjoyed a post-meal cigar at their table as Frankie watched the revival staff busily prepare for the upcoming healing service.

Amos Tilley approached and asked, "Get plenty?"

Frankie nodded. His father spat a piece of tobacco over his shoulder.

"Y'all stickin' round for the rest of the service?"

"No, thank you very much," Jameson replied haughtily. He tilted his head back and released a stream of smoke.

"Well, if you change your mind... I tell you, that boy, Teddy Watkins, he's for real. The Lord surely works through him in ama—"

"Hate I'll miss it," Jameson said.

"I've seen him heal deformities...bring sight to the blind." Amos leaned close to Jameson's ear. "Maybe let him lay hands on Frankie? I'm tellin' ya, Frank, God blesses his people with spiritual gifts. That boy has the gift of heal—"

"You believe this shit, do ya? What 'bout your wife, Amos? Why didn't you get miracle boy to make her well? Huh?"

Amos straightened and stuck his hands in his pockets.

Jameson frowned. "Hell. I'm sorry."

"Forget it, Frank," Amos said, taking a step back. "I'll check on y'all come mornin'."

"'Preciate the meal," Jameson replied dryly.

Amos gave Frankie a friendly wink. He squeezed the boy's shoulder and whispered, "Sleep well, now. Don't let the coyotes get ya."

Frankie's eyes widened.

Amos snorted and patted Frankie's back. When the farmer left to visit another table, Frankie stood, expecting they'd return to their campsite. But his father remained seated. Through the cigar smoke, Jameson watched a couple of men carry tall stacks of white buckets into the tent. On the bottom bucket, the word *OFFERING* was hand-painted in large, uppercase lettering.

Jameson stubbed out his cigar on the edge of the table and let the butt fall to the ground. Rising to his feet, faithless Frank Jameson announced, "Let's stick around. Give this healin' production a day in court."

• • •

A man hurried to the center of the stage where Evangelist Herman Roscoe stood in his immaculate white suit. He handed Roscoe a piece of paper. He then left the stage in the same brisk stride.

"We have a man with us today," Roscoe solemnly proclaimed into his microphone. "His back..." He paced the stage as he read. "For three years, he's had tremendous pain in his back. The discs...they are... The discs are misaligned." Roscoe made a wavy line with the hand holding the note. "And the doctors say the surgery needed to straighten his back could likely leave him permanently paralyzed."

The note bearer reemerged, moving much more slowly as he guided a middle-aged man, nearly doubled over, by the arm.

Teddy Watkins stood, turned to set his Bible on the seat of his chair, and stepped out to join Roscoe. Frankie guessed Teddy to be about his own age, eleven, maybe twelve. He seemed an exact miniature of Herman Roscoe. He wore a white suit, white shirt, white shoes, with a black tie and handkerchief. His sandy-blonde pompadour was combed back in waves. Only his diminutive stature and cherubic face belied his authoritative aura.

Roscoe stuffed the note into his jacket pocket. "Brother Teddy...this fine man, this proud man... He can no longer work to provide for his family," Roscoe informed the boy as if he'd not been sitting ten feet away during the preliminary summation. "Why, any man can't feed his family is sure to feel less than a man."

Jameson snorted in his chair, his legs splayed, arms crossed above his shiny belt buckle.

The escort stepped away but remained on the stage, facing the congregation with his arms behind his back. Roscoe addressed the impaired man directly, "You say you have excruciating pain in your back?"

"Yes, sir. Terrible."

Roscoe shot Teddy Watkins a glance. The boy returned a knowing nod.

"And you can't do your job at the plant on account of the toll it takes on you? You can't do the liftin' that's required of you?"

"No sir, can't—"

"And therefore, you were fired, and you haven't been able to provide for your family. To feed and clothe them like you'd faithfully done before this pain took over?"

"That's right, sir. Our kids...they gotta get their clothes from—"

"Turn 'round for me." Roscoe maneuvered the man so that his arched back faced the congregation. "This man has lost his ability to use his body, folks. But he's not lost his faith in the ability of his Lord Jesus Christ. If he had, he wouldn't be here now, would he?"

A murmur of affirmation.

"Brother Teddy," Roscoe said. He wedged the microphone into his armpit. Then, he stepped aside and gestured to the boy to take over. Teddy Watkins began to move both hands up and down the man's spine.

"Folks, I have no doubt the Lord is sending his healing power through the hands of his faithful servant into this man's crooked back," Roscoe announced. "Praise God, I know it's straightenin' as I speak. Brother Teddy, can you feel it being restored beneath the very palms of your hands, Amen?"

Teddy Watkins nodded, his small hands still working.

"The discs realignin' to their rightful order?"

"They are," the boy confirmed.

Suddenly, Teddy Watkins jerked away as if he'd touched

a hot stove. With his palms raised to the congregation, he declared, "It is done!"

"Folks, the Lord has healed this man," Roscoe declared. "I know it to be true." He hurriedly spun the man around to face the congregation. "How's your back feel, sir?"

The man stood tall, a wide grin on his face. "Feels good. Pain's gone. I can straight—"

"Did you hear that, folks? The pain is completely gone." Roscoe eyed the man. "Is that right?"

"It's gone," the man corroborated.

Roscoe scanned the crowd with wide eyes. "Brethren, God has healed this man right here under this humble tent tonight."

A chorus of amens erupted.

He took the healed man's hand and raised it into the air. "Now the doubters would say, 'How do we know it's really healed?' Folks, I weigh one hundred and eighty-two pounds." He glanced over his shoulder at those on the stage behind him. "Now, I was at one seventy-five before that wonderful meal we shared earlier. Amen?"

Nods and laughter.

"Sir, how'd you like to show these folks what God has done for you tonight?"

"Yes. I wanna show 'em what God done for me."

"How 'bout you lift me up in your arms. That'll show 'em. Why, when you first walked over to me, you were all bent over, ain't that so?" Roscoe mimicked the man's pre-healing gait. He straightened and stuck the microphone in the man's face.

"Yes, sir," he replied, throwing his shoulders back proudly. "Now I'm standing straight 'n tall."

"Watch this, folks." Again, Roscoe secured the microphone under his arm. He shouted to the man, "Pick me up. Go ahead."

The man lifted the evangelist off the ground and set him back on his feet.

"Again!" Roscoe yelled.

The man lifted him, then lowered him to the stage.

"Again!"

The man began repeatedly hoisting Roscoe into the air. The evangelist hooted and laughed hysterically. The piano started up, and Roscoe and the healed man began dancing around the stage, their arms flailing. Teddy Watkins pumped his fist, smiling triumphantly. When the song ended, the man continued his celebration until Roscoe lightly pushed him away. The escort quickly stepped forward and hurried the restored man off the stage.

There were many others. A lady regained her hearing. Cancerous tumors were expelled from one elderly man. A woman's defective arm, which had hung limply at her hip as she was led across the stage, was made healthy again. This miracle was confirmed with Roscoe kneeling on one knee and cranking the limb as if it were the handle of a well pump. Another man shot out of the deathbed his brother had wheeled to the foot of the stage. Between healings, songs of praise were performed. There was clapping and dancing in the aisles, with Roscoe's tambourine rattling in a celebratory blur.

With resounding hope, Frankie stared up at his father, parted his mouth, and put a finger to his lip. Jameson rolled his head toward him, then away. "You ever wanna talk, then talk, boy," he chided. "Don't waste time waitin' 'round for no miracle. You open your goddamn mouth and speak." Immediately, Frankie felt the tears well up, but he fought them back.

Frank Jameson hadn't allowed his family to attend church. But after losing his mother four years earlier, young Frankie began having conversations in his own head. One-sided as they were, he nonetheless felt that whoever he was silently pleading to was listening. He'd received no audible replies, no visible signs to convince him of such. And his existence within this world had not improved. Moreover, since having to join his father on his precarious travels, life had grown considerably more chaotic, confusing, and frightening. But in these private moments, there was a physical sensation, a slight flutter within his chest, that always brought a smile to his typically stoic face.

At last, the music ended, and Roscoe stepped to the edge of the stage wiping his face with the towel. "For all the Lord has done here tonight, we ask that you do something for *him*. Before we bid our farewells and go off to get a good night's rest, some folks are gonna pass around the offerin' buckets. The money you give, it don't go in my pocket. It don't go in Brother Teddy's pocket neither. If it did, he'd have him a lifetime supply of Hershey chocolate bars. Amen, brother?" There was laughter as the boy nodded excitedly, his eyes wide. "What your gift does is get us to the next town so we can keep on saving souls, glorifyin' Christ, and healin' the sick. So, while we praise God up here with one last song, will you good folks praise him with your tithes and offerings so we can continue spreadin' his word on down the road?"

Jameson turned to his son. "Wonder why they don't just pray for the buckets to fill themselves?"

Roscoe began singing the first verse of a hymn. The piano quickly caught up and soon, the others onstage were singing and clapping as nicely dressed men went row by row, passing the two-gallon buckets. When the loaded bucket reached his father's hands, Frankie watched him raise and lower it as if weighing it with his arms, his covetous eyes tallying its contents. Finally, Jameson passed it on, having affected neither its weight nor worth.

When it had made its way to the end of the row, another man took it and carried it by its handle down the outside aisle. Frankie watched his father track the bucket's path. The offering handlers gathered in front of the stage until the last of them arrived. Then, they carried the buckets to a flatbed truck parked outside the tent. Each man deposited his charge onto the truck bed. Another man, younger, dressed in casual clothing and wearing a cap, secured the wooden tailgate and climbed into the cab.

Frankie watched the truck descend the path that led to the wooded campsite. In the moonlight, he saw movement inside a big wire cage under the truck's back window. He thought of the monkey cage which now sat empty in the truck trailer. One morning, his father's flea-riddled mascot had cavalierly scooped up a mound of its own fresh feces and slung it into his master's face. Consequently, Monty the Monkey had gone missing later in the day, and Jameson performed his duties at that night's show with infected eyes nearly swollen shut.

Jameson nodded toward the truck as it disappeared into the pine forest. "Hell, that kind of scratch could get *us* on down the road too." He turned to Frankie and arched his brow. "I figure some of that belongs to me anyways. Seein' how it should've been *my* tent pitched in this field stead of these holy rollers."

Frankie shot him a concerned look. "Close them saucers, boy," Jameson chided. "I'm funnin' ya."

"Before we leave here tonight, I want y'all to stand and look my way." It was Teddy Watkins. He motioned for the crowd to rise. "Everyone on their feet," he said in a high pre-pubescent voice. "Every head turn this way. Every eye on me. I want y'all to do somethin'...it's gonna be real easy. I want you to say his name. Jesus. Just say his name. Out loud or to yourselves. Jesus. That's all there is to it. If you got a hurt. A pain. A disease. You got a part of your body ain't workin' right. Don't need to tell him what it is. He knows. Look at me and say his name. Jesus."

Frankie couldn't see the stage, only the rears of folks standing in front of him. He craned his neck and stood on the tips of his toes to no avail. Eventually, he gave up and stood still with his arms hanging at his sides. Then, through the murmur of "Jesus. Jesus. Jesus," he heard a voice say, "Look at me, Frankie."

Frankie jerked his head toward his father, but Jameson was hunched forward in his chair, busily carving his fingernails with a pocketknife, letting the trimmings fall between his splayed legs.

"Look at me, Frankie," came the gentle command again. Frankie looked around him, but all were facing forward and whispering obediently. Finally, he turned and climbed onto the seat of his chair. When he stood, stretching tall, he had a clear view of the boy evangelist, whose arms were crossed over the Bible held against his chest. He was staring directly at Frankie, whose head was now level with the rest of the congregation. In that moment, something stirred in Frankie's chest. It was the hopefulness that his father had dashed mere moments earlier. The same feeling as when his mother would tuck him into bed at night. When it was just the two of them. After his father had passed out and the dogs had stopped barking. It was the feeling that everything would be all right. That he was safe. Like when Jarvis had been alive. His huge peaceful presence. The way the giant man winked at him, letting him know that no harm would come to him. It was the feeling that someone was watching over him.

The singular beautiful name of Jesus flooded Frankie's mind as he and the boy healer remained joined in mysterious union. Then, Frankie heard, "He hears you. You will be okay."

Soon, members of the congregation began turning to see where Little Teddy's focus was drawn to. Frankie, standing frozen on the chair, became aware of the sea of faces looking his way.

"Get yer ass down off that." Jameson grabbed his son's arm and yanked him off the chair. Frankie fell forward, hitting his head on the seat rest of the chair in front of him. "Damned clumsy fool," Jameson growled under his breath.

Frankie stared up at his father with a serene expression that slowly grew into a wide smile.

"Hell, boy. If you ain't the squirreliest young'un I ever seen," Jameson said, pulling Frankie up by his shirt sleeve. "Let's beat feet outta here."

• • •

Back at the campsite, there was no sign of the others. Near the shore sat a pile of unburned sticks and branches and an overturned cook pot. The van's back door swung open. Lois jumped to the ground and stood with her hands on her hips.

"Wood won't light," she said in her angry voice, which sounded as if she'd taken a shot of helium. "It's still damp from the rain."

"Hell, woman," Jameson blurted, "them beans is done cooked when they put 'em in the can. You can eat 'em cold good as warm. If you're too damned highfalutin to eat cold beans, then get your little ass back in the van and go hungry."

Lois turned and stomped away, followed by the sound of the van's door slamming closed.

A fishy yet mercifully cool breeze wafted off the lake and through the cab's open windows. Frankie lay by his father in the cramped sleeper compartment, his mind replaying that night's event under the revival tent before dozing off. At some point during the night, Frankie heard the truck door open and close softly. He quickly fell back to sleep.

In a dream, Frankie sees the tree twinkling in the corner of their ramshackle living room. Smells the spilled beer in the fabric of the tattered couch that served as his bed. Hears his mother's cry followed by a deafening explosion. The ringing in his ears. The bloodstain on his mother's nightgown when he comes upon her in the hallway. His father's dark threatening eyes fixed on him. Police officers nodding to the words "burglar" and "terrible accident." Wanting to scream, "Liar!"

When Frankie awoke again, dawn had come. He raised himself enough to look through the window. After rubbing his vision clear with the heels of his hands, he could make out his father's figure, cigar in hand, pacing the shoreline. After a short time, Jameson blew smoke into the misty air and flicked the butt into the water. Then, he brought his right hand close to his face. He wiggled his fingers and opened and closed the hand several times.

Frankie climbed into the passenger seat and watched his father approach.

"I'll be goddamned," Jameson said, studying his hand from every angle. He glanced up and noticed Frankie's face in the open window. "You need to pee?"

Frankie nodded.

"Go water a tree, we're headin' out. Gonna make a couple of stops on our way up to Partonsburg."

Frankie did his business. As he came out of the woods belting his trousers, he heard Lois call to him, "Hi, Frankie." He returned a sheepish smile.

She and the twins were drinking steaming coffee from little tin cups.

Frankie glanced back at the pile of unburned wood.

"Amos brought us a whole kettleful," Lois exclaimed proudly.

"Frankie boy," Jeb yelled. "We all seen your tally whacker."

Frankie felt his face warm.

"Hush, Jeb," Lois said.

"Stop your jabberin' and get your asses in the van," Jameson said, coming toward them.

Frankie hurried to the truck.

"Fair's a week out. I got a few stops in mind on route."

• • •

"Listen up, boy," Jameson said, lighting a fresh cigar. "You gonna play it just like that hallelujah gig. Only we ain't gonna waste hours healin' everyone right there on the stage. One live healin' per group, ya hear?"

"He can't talk, Frank," Lois said wryly.

Jameson glowered at her; Lois returned a smirk.

"I'll pick out one mark per show, get him up onto the stage so everybody gets a good look at him... Hears his story."

"Or hers," Lois added.

"Hush it," Jameson snapped.

They were huddled inside the newly christened Healing

Tent. Jameson was objectively "framin' the show," as he called it; the first aimed at selling his latest elixir. They'd traveled thirty miles north of Olivia to a town Jameson had visited many times during his patent medicine and amusement tenure. It was an isolated region whose unwitting population still welcomed any sort of entertainment with credulous enthusiasm.

"And that's how it's gonna go," Jameson decreed, his intense eyes flitting from face to face.

All returned hesitant nods.

"Best you perk up," Jameson said. "We was 'bout to fold up the tent for good. Then where'd ya be? Not a big demand for potion makes you sing off-key or tell stale one-liners. Couple of howlin' hillbillies and a not-too-funny runt ain't gonna move product. We was lucky havin' Jarvis. He was the real goods. Folks look at him, see his power, they gonna buy what he's sellin'. And Samuel, the deserter. You got an eighty-year-old man onstage flashin' his nine-inch steel pipe, you damn sure gonna sell potency potion to every droopin' codger in town. This angel boy thing, folks gonna see it happen right before their eyes...and they gonna want it for themselves." Jameson turned to the boy. "What 'bout you? You understand how things gonna run tonight?"

"He can't talk, Dr. Frank," Lois repeated with obvious annoyance.

Jameson flashed Lois a scowl. "Gimme that." He snatched up the costume draped over Lois's outstretched arms. He shook his head as he studied it.

"Done the best I could with them wings," she stated defensively. "That ol' trader you sent me to didn't have no bleached feathers. I traded for what he had and coated 'em with dustin' powder."

Jameson scoffed. "I never said he sold no white feathers, did I? Said he sold feathers. That's what I said."

Lois's hands balled into pudgy fists at her sides. She exhaled and continued, "I went a little over on measurements so he can grow with it."

Jameson clamped the cigar between his brown teeth and held the suit up to Frankie. "Hell, woman. Damn thing's gonna swaller him up." He raised his head to the sky. "God sends his healin' angel down wrapped in ill-fittin' clothes. Ain't that just golden?"

"Make it yourself then," Lois replied, tossing a small white masquerade mask at her boss's boots.

Jameson stuck his finger in Lois's taut, defiant face. "I won't forget that one, little lady."

Frankie felt his gut begin to stir.

Jameson picked up the mask and blew on it. "Now, once they catch sight of that one genuine healin', we herd 'em out to the merch table and start movin' them bottles. Take their money, give 'em their cures, and send 'em on their way. Got it?"

More nods.

Jameson's expression revealed little faith in his subordinates. He threw his hands in the air, then turned to the open back doors of the truck trailer and announced, "Showtime, baby Jesus."

Teddy Watkins sat cross-legged inside the padlocked cage that had once been home to Monty, the rogue monkey. The corner of a red handkerchief, the very one Jameson used to dry sweat from his face and clear his nasal cavities, hung from the boy's mouth. Frankie stood beside his father, looking into Teddy's bright blue eyes. He mouthed the word *Sorry*.

Jameson removed a set of keys from the pocket of his

trousers and hurriedly worked the padlock open. He grabbed the boy's arm and pulled him close. "You best deliver them healings, boy. You don't, God can't save ya from what *I'm* gonna deliver. You hear?"

"Yes," Teddy said, smiling into his captor's face.

After a moment of holding the boy's gaze, Jameson said, "Don't look at me like that, boy. Like you pullin' one over on me." He roughly worked the mask onto the boy's face. "I'm your master now. Hear? You just my little miracle monkey."

"Yes," Teddy said.

The new canvas banner boasted the bold, arched heading "HEALING BOY ANGEL" followed in smaller lettering by "DR. FRANK'S HEAVENLY HEALING SERUM." The paint was fresh and vibrant, its illustration wildly animated: a boy—whose euphoric countenance the artist modeled from a children's clothing ad Jameson had torn from a magazine—dressed in white from head to toe, soared among the cumulus clouds high above rolling green mountains, his huge wings in full expanse, his chubby little hands holding an amber bottle emitting bright rays of light.

From the side of the bally stage, Frankie watched his father deliver his spiel. Jameson had learned the "talk" as a young apprentice to his own father, Frank Jameson Sr., who started "The Dr. Frank Show" after returning from the first war. Frank Jr. delivered a fervent, if not well-articulated, pitch. "That's right, folks," he shouted into the microphone while waving his cane at the exaggerated angel boy banner. "This evenin', for the very first time, you can bear witness to a real-life miracle. An angel boy, sent downward from the heavenly parts to do the Lord's work through acts of supernatural healin'. Hear me now. One real-life healin' per group performed in front of your very eyes. All you gotta do is buy your ticket and follow the lovely Ms. Lois McGhee into the Healing Tent to behold the wonder of it."

There was ambivalent murmuring among Jameson's potential tips.

"Now, who here would like to be considered to receive the live healin' tonight?"

The murmurs increased in volume. Jameson walked the length of the stage, scanning the hesitant faces.

"I got this lump on my neck," came a strange voice from the crowd.

"Step forward, mister," Dr. Frank called out, lifting his chin, his dark eyes searching. "C'mon up, now. Let me get a gander at ya."

The crowd parted to let the man through. When he'd made it to the foot of the stage, he looked up to Jameson with a pleading countenance. The growth on the side of his neck was the size of an orange.

"Pain's somethin' awful," the man said, each word sounding like a croak from a frog. "Doc says it's pushin' on some nerves. Says it's no use him cuttin' on it."

"That so?" Dr. Frank replied with a serious guise.

"Yep," the man said, running the palm of his hand over the lump. He cleared his throat loudly. "Now...you tellin' me that angel boy can make this go away?"

"I'm tellin' you and all the good folks standing before me who'd like to come inside to verify it. This boy, this angel, was sent to earth with the power from God to heal those who *believe*."

The man with the protruding growth scanned the faces of those around him. "And it ain't to cost me a penny, you say?"

"Not for that one fortunate soul who believes enough to

step into that tent behind us and take a walk of faith right up to the platform in front of all these witnesses." Jameson grinned. "Now...for you others, a ticket to *witness* the healing is but a single dime. Afterwards, you'll have an opportunity to purchase, at a very reasonable fee, a bottle of our miracle serum. It's done been prayed over by the healin' angel boy and infused with God's restoration power. There ain't no limit to the number of bottles you can procure. So you be thinkin' of them loved ones that ain't here tonight. Them that is down with back pain, doubled over with stomach ailments, struck lame with the arthritis..."

There was groaning from the crowd.

"Now listen up, folks. Listen to me good. No more payin' for them useless doctor visits. No more prescription costs. All you gotta do is truly believe in the work of God on them bottles back there."

The groaning intensified. Frankie felt his face warm with concern.

"Now, the money you bestow here tonight for the unique opportunity to witness a real-life healin'. For the chance to take home a bottle of genuine miracle serum. That money don't go into my pocket. If it did, you better believe I'd have me a lifetime supply of them Cuban imports." Jameson closed his eyes and mimicked puffing on a cigar, then blew imaginary smoke into the air.

Frankie felt a twinge of relief when he noticed a few grins in the sea of faces.

"So, what *does* your humble token go toward, you may wonder? Why, it simply allows us to travel on to the next town so we can keep helpin' folks in need of healin.'"

It took nearly forty-five minutes for Dr. Frank to encourage enough curiosity seekers to fill the Healing Tent for the first show, or "turn the tip," as it was called in the AB. An anxious Jameson handed the microphone over to the Harpeth Twins before joining Frankie inside the tent. Outside, Frankie could hear Pokey and Jeb performing a cappella one of the Gospel hymns they had recently worked up to complement the show's revised theme. Inside the dark, humid tent packed with sweaty bodies and a sense of guarded anticipation, Frankie felt his heart beating wildly in his chest. It was as if his body had forgotten its innate duty, leaving him to deliberately fight for each breath.

Teddy Watkins stood on the platform. The boy angel's crudely constructed wings, which Lois had sewn into the shoulders of his white suit jacket, hung limply at his sides. Loose feathers gathered around his polished white patent leather shoes.

The man with the goiter ascended the steps and stood between Lois and Teddy. Lois put the microphone to her mouth and announced, "This man has a tumor on his neck that—"

"No shit!" came a shout from the crowd.

Laughter erupted. Frankie glanced up to see his father nervously stroking his thick mustache.

Under a bare light bulb, Little Lois's rouged cheeks grew redder. "Our angel," Lois said, shooting a look at Teddy Watkins, who turned and took the bottle from a white cloth-covered table behind them, "will now take normal everyday water and infuse it with the healing power given to him directly by God."

Teddy Watkins held the bottle with both hands and brought it to his chest, his blue eyes gleaming behind the mask. After a few seconds, he handed the medicine bottle to

Lois, who held it up to the crowd with trembling hands, her expression filled with simulated awe. She opened her mouth to speak, then smiled awkwardly and handed the bottle to the afflicted man. Teddy Watkins glanced up and noticed tears streaming down into the deep creases of his cheeks. He whispered, "Drink it."

"Drink it, fella," came a shout from the crowd. Then a chorus of, "Drink it! Drink it!"

Frankie noticed little Teddy Watkins's blue eyes brighten inside the leather eye mask as the man turned up the bottle. By the time he'd emptied its contents, the mass had vanished altogether.

Jameson grabbed his son's arm and squeezed, causing Frankie to wince. "Goddamnit, boy," Jameson whispered, his eyes scanning the backs of the thirty-some heads, "I'm gonna be rollin' in it."

•••

The carnival site was a sprawling field at the base of the mountains just outside the burgeoning resort town of Partonsburg. Frankie had always loved this area. The air was cooler, and the rolling hills looked as if they were covered in a thick green blanket.

Already there was activity. Trucks and campers were parked along the perimeter. Folks were milling about, erecting various structures along what would form the midway. A man waved them over. Jameson eased the rig up to him and cranked the half-open window the rest of the way down. He shouted over the truck's rumbling engine, "You in charge?"

"That's what they tell me," the man replied with a wide grin. "Name?"

"Frank Jameson Jr."

"Afternoon, Mr. Jameson. License?"

Jameson stuck the crinkled paper in the man's face. "Where do ya got me?" Jameson asked curtly.

The man checked his clipboard, then turned and pointed. "Right along there, sir."

Jameson nodded. "How's the weather lookin'?"

"Calm and clear...straight through the weekend," the man answered. He looked into the cloudless sky and said, "Thank you, Jesus."

Jameson grunted. "There come a blow down, I'll be lookin' for ya."

The man let out an uneasy chuckle.

They'd worked the show in three different towns without a hitch and sold every last pint of healing water. Jameson had to send the twins out scavenging for a new supply in preparation for a five-night run at the big fair. "We're gonna make a killin' in Partonsburg," had become his mantra.

Frankie took his customary stance at the side of the bally stage and watched his father work the growing crowd. When Jameson began pitching for the first free healing of the night, he was met with an immediate response. "Right here!"

Dr. Frank jerked his head in the direction of the voice. "I hear ya. I hear ya. Move closer now so I can lay eyes on ya."

Two middle-aged men, both wearing long beards, bullied their way through the bodies. It was not until they arrived at the foot of the stage that Jameson noticed the much older man with them. He was a head shorter than his two burly cohorts. One side of his face was discolored, and a large area of missing hair was evident above his misshapen ear. One of the bearded men called up, "This is our daddy. His name is

Jacob Hess. He was servin' the good people of this county many years back. This was the thanks he got." Then he grabbed his father's wrist and raised his arm into the air. The old man's mangled hand resembled the crusher claw of a lobster. The fingers and skin had melded into a single reddish mass. A tiny appendage, short and straight, protruded from where a thumb would have been.

Every face gazed in restrained revulsion at the old man's deformity.

"Looks like we got some kind of burn, do we?" Jameson ventured. "About the face and—"

"And this little thing stickin' out come off his foot," the son said over Jameson. "It's useless. Doctor stuck one of his toes on there for looks."

The other son pointed to the canvas banner and said, "If that angel boy can't fix this mess back like yer a claimin' he can, then yer nuthin' but a damned heretic." He turned to face the crowd. "Either our daddy gets healed, or they's doin' the Devil's work. Claimin' false miracles in the name of God Almighty."

This declaration brought about an uncomfortable silence. Frankie felt a wave of nausea roll through him. He watched his father hover over the three men, leaning on the cane he held in his right hand. Jameson opened and closed his grip on its curved silver-plated handle, straightened his fingers, then squeezed until his knuckles went white.

"I believe we've found our first public healin' of the night," Jameson declared into his microphone. Jacob Hess received the enthusiastic announcement with an unblinking, dead-eyed glower aimed at Dr. Frank.

Frankie watched anxiously from the back of the Healing

Tent. Enmity permeated the sweltering atmosphere. He could sense that this group was nothing like the crowds they'd had at the last few stops.

Standing at the foot of the stage were the two sons with their long, ragged beards. Teddy Watkins took his position on the platform. On his right was the feeble but feisty Jacob Hess. Next to Hess was Little Lois donning a shabby white headdress and belted tunic. The attire, procured at Jameson's behest, gave her the appearance of a mythic goblin rather than that of a faithful convert following her messiah along the dusty thoroughfares of old Jerusalem. The microphone she held, which emitted continuous and unnerving feedback, did little to bolster the Biblical-times aura.

"Pokey," Lois spoke into the microphone, prompting an earsplitting squawk.

Pokey leapt onto the stage and began adjusting knobs on the loudspeaker. He gave Lois a nod.

Lois held the microphone away from her face. "Testing, testing." She turned and gave Pokey a thumbs-up. "Good. We're good, now," she said reservedly.

"Get on with it," one of the Hess boys hollered.

"Yes, well," Lois began, "we want to thank all y'all for being here to witness the first live healing of the night. This is Mr. Jacob Hess standing before you. And...and as you can see..." Lois gently placed her free hand on the old man's cheek. Hess knocked her arm away with his deformed appendage.

"I don't care 'bout my looks, little missy. I'm eighty-six years old. Ain't gonna be enterin' no beauty contest."

"Oh...oookay...well..." Lois stammered.

The very air inside the small tent seemed to thicken. Not a single person moved, the only sound being the ambient noise coming from the midway beyond.

Hess raised the bum hand over his head. "I want this angel boy to fix this here calamity. So's I can use it again. I want my old hand back. I lost it doin' the Lord's work. Don't reckon it's too much to ask him for it back. That's what the sparklin' clown out there said you can do. So you best start provin' it."

At this, a nervous giggle escaped into the microphone, causing another burst of feedback.

"I say somethin' funny, darlin'?" Hess said, glaring down at Lois, his brow furrowed in contempt.

"No, sir, mister—"

"Ain't no comedy in losin' use of a hand tryin' to uphold the laws of the Almighty."

"Is that boy gonna heal our daddy or not?" his other son called out impatiently.

Hess lowered his arm toward Teddy Watkins. His eyes scanned the faces in the crowd with a sinister expression that said, *Let's see what he's got.*

Teddy grasped the forearm with both hands. He shot a quick glance at the man's sons, then his eyes shifted to Frankie standing at the back of the tent. Frankie watched Teddy's blue eyes grow luminous behind the mask. As they held each other's gaze, Frankie heard a voice. "God knows a man's heart and his actions, Frankie. He knows his future and his past." Then, as if the two boys' individual consciousness had somehow coupled, the shared vision commenced.

Jacob Hess carries a torch as he leads the way down the dark wooded path. Following behind him, a couple of his brethren are wielding revolvers. Another carries a bottle in each hand with a gasoline-soaked rag sticking out of its punctured lid. His vision is limited to that which is visible through the holes cut out of the white hood he wears over his head, fastened around his neck by a length of rope. They come upon a clearing where a two-story wood-planked house sits darkly still under the moonless sky. They move to the front of the house and climb the steps onto the porch. In the torchlight, Hess notices the nail and paper fragment stuck to the front door where his crudely written warning notice had been torn away.

"We give 'em their two weeks," he reminds his comrades crowding in behind him.

"What 'bout the young'uns?" one of them asks.

"Like I said, we give 'em fair warnin'." Hess bangs the fisted heel of his free hand on the door. "We done give ya yer warnin'. All you whores leave now. C'mon out. We gonna step aside, let you pass. No harm'll come to ya. Time you and yer brood of bastard young'uns leave these parts."

There is no reply from inside the house. The only sounds are those of the visiting locusts and the soles of muddy boots scooting around on the porch floor. Hess lowers his torch, illuminating the doorknob. Just as he wraps his fingers around its rusted surface, an explosion comes from behind the door. The force of the blast sends a section of splintered board slamming into Hess's arm. The torch meets the side of his head. He drops it just as another blast comes. The man carrying the two bottle grenades folds onto the floor. Hess feels the instant heat and hears the crackling of singed hair, clothing, and skin. He sees nothing but raging flames through the eye holes.

The voice returned. "Nothing happens that's not part of his plan, Frankie." Frankie kept his eyes fixed on those of Teddy Watkins, still beaming inside the mask. "Watch."

Frankie sees his father staggering among the tall trunks of mist-shrouded pines. It's the wooded area on the perimeter of Amos Tilley's farm. Teddy Watkins suddenly appears. "That goddamn dog got me," Jameson cries out, breathing erratically. "The pig-eyed fucker!" Frankie sees the horrific image of his father's hand, the torn flesh hanging loosely from exposed bones, severed veins spilling blood onto the white bucket overturned at his feet. Without hesitation or solicitation, without touch, and most certainly without an ounce of faith from the beneficiary, Teddy restores the hand until there is no evidence of the quick and violent attack. Next, Frankie sees his father stuffing a bandana into Teddy's mouth. Then, with no resistance from his captor, Jameson drags the boy back to their campsite and locks him in the monkey cage kept inside the stifling truck trailer.

Frankie comes out of the dreamlike vision with his heart pounding in his chest, his wide eyes still locked on those of Teddy Watkins.

"What the hell's goin' on with you, angel boy?" one of Hess's sons shouted. "You ain't gonna do what you say you can do?"

"If you ain't," the other warned, "then we got us a problem here."

Teddy stood still, saying nothing, continuing to stare at Frankie, his blue eyes gleaming.

Jacob Hess glanced down at the winged healer; his disfigured face grew more distorted as a scowl enveloped it. "Back in the day, boy..." he whispered. "Yer kind? Doin' the Devil's work under the blessed name of Almighty God? We'd've likely given yer back a good lashin'. Maybe till yer ribs showed through the torn flesh. Then we'd flip ya over and give yer front a good coat of tar. And them phony wings yer wearin'? We'd pluck 'em off into a wash basin, then empty it all over ya. Hell, might even've strapped ya to a mule and paraded ya through the middle of town...let ev'ryone know the fate of an evil doer." Hess whistled. "White Caps knowed how to make an example of yer kind, boy."

Cries of "Heal him!" and "Scam!" came from the enlivening crowd.

Frankie darted out of the tent and bolted up the steps of the bally stage. He yanked on the sleeve of his father's sparkling jacket, interrupting his pitch for the second show.

Jameson moved the microphone away from his face and whispered nastily, "What the hell you want, boy?"

Frankie pointed frantically.

Jameson dashed into the tent with his son on his bootheels. Frankie stopped just inside and watched his father push his way through the sweaty crowd. He stopped directly between the Hess brothers at the foot of the stage. He raised his cane and pressed its tip into Teddy's midsection. "Boooyyy," he growled, "if you don't heal this gentleman, quick like, then you best start flappin' them wings and hope they get ya far 'way from the likes of me."

Teddy remained motionless and silent. He once again fixed his bright unblinking eyes on Frankie. A slight grin formed on his plump red lips.

Jameson turned and glowered at his son, then started toward him. But as he charged away from the stage, one of the towering Hess brothers clamped an arm over his shoulder, stopping him cold.

He screamed into Jameson's ear, "Where the hell you think you're goin'?" His glare swept over the crowd. "Him and that boy's runnin' a scam on us here," he shouted while struggling to keep Jameson in his grip, "and they's doin' it in God's name."

"Blasphemy!" came one exclamation, followed by, "You stole from us!"

Frankie saw the transformation in his father's face, the features twisting into a sinister grimace. Jameson writhed out of Hess's grasp and tried to run. But the second Hess brother quickly shoved him in the back, propelling him forward as he stumbled to the ground. In a matter of seconds, a group of men had encircled him. "I'll fuckin' kill ever last one of ya," Jameson growled.

The Hesses began kicking Jameson as he rolled in the dirt trying to protect himself. Some joined in the physical abuse, while others began spitting and shouting verbal threats at him. Several folks, mostly women and children, rushed past Frankie as they made for the exit.

A thunderous explosion instantly silenced all noise and stopped all movement inside the tent. On the vacated stage stood Jeb Harpeth, his mouth drawn tight, his shoulders rolling with each heavy breath, his legs set in a wide stance, the muzzle of Frank Jameson's beloved Remington 1900 aimed skyward. "Get the fuck outta here. All you'uns. Now!"

Jeb commanded. "I ain't had much schoolin', but I can count to two." He glanced up at the slivers of canvas hanging from the jagged perimeter of a hole the twelve-gauge round had made. "That there's one," he said. Then slowly, dramatically, he leveled the twin barrels at the group of agitators hovering over his whimpering boss.

• • •

Lois sat on the edge of the platform inside the Healing Tent, her pudgy bare feet dangling over the edge. Jameson's battered head lay in her lap. She was working to stop the stream of blood pouring from Jameson's nose.

He groaned as he lightly touched his abdomen with the tips of his fingers. "There ain't much can be done 'bout that, Frank," Lois said. "Pain'll pass with time."

Jameson scoffed.

"You think them Hess men gonna call the law?" Jeb asked Pokey, who'd just returned from another security check.

"Hell no, they ain't," Pokey said. "We got physical assault on 'em."

Jameson winced as he tried to rise. Lois laid her hand on his shoulder and eased him back down. He aimed a finger at Jeb, who'd been pacing in front of the stage and mumbling incessantly.

Jeb stopped in his tracks. "What?" he said warily.

"You ever lay a hand on my shotgun again..."

Jeb brought his fists to his hips. "Fine, boss. Next time, I'll let 'em kill ya."

Jameson jerked his head up.

"Back down, Frank!" Lois snapped.

He stared at her incredulously, then shot hateful glances at the others. "What the hell's goin' on with all y'all? You think I won't whup every one of yer damned asses on account of some sore ribs?"

"Take it easy, Frank," Lois said softly. She parted the blood-matted hair on the side of his head. "Boot toe gotcha good here."

Jameson pushed her hand away. "You wanna fix me up, nurse? Get yer sausages outta my hair and bring me somethin' to stop this goddamn achin.'"

Lois gave the twins a look. She then flashed a sympathetic grin at Frankie, who sat cross-legged on the stage next to her.

Jameson took a slow, deep breath and let it out. "Where's the boy?"

"He..." Jeb began, then threw his hands up. "We don't know, boss."

"Don't know?" Jameson mocked. He aimed his penetrating eyes up at Lois. "You?"

Lois shook her head.

"You want me to go lookin' for him, boss?" Pokey asked.

"There's an idea," Jameson said, then let out a sigh. "No. Leave it be."

"Leave it be?" Lois said, the divergence evident. "He's a boy, Frank."

Jameson scoffed. "You real sure 'bout that?"

Frankie quietly fiddled with his bootstring while pondering his father's remark.

"You need directions, woman?" Jameson growled. "Get me some medicine. I'm a hurtin' here!"

Lois quickly scooted out from under Jameson, leaving his bleeding head to drop onto the plywood floor with a thud. She hoisted herself off the stage and onto the dirt ground, then stomped out of the tent.

No one spoke in Lois's absence. When she returned, she held an amber-colored glass bottle clenched in one hand. She handed it to Jameson, who snatched it from her, then let out a long groan as he eased himself up. He unscrewed the lid and took a generous pull. After a moment of labored breathing, he took another just as Pokey came rushing into the tent. "They're comin'."

Jameson pushed himself off the stage, landing on his feet with an agonizing yowl. He staggered to the exit and pulled back the canvas flap. Frankie rushed up behind him and took a quick one-eyed peek from around his waist. In the early morning darkness, he saw tiny bouncing balls of fire at the far end of the vacant midway. As the flaming spheres drew nearer, he could make out the images of several men holding torches in their outstretched hands.

"Y'all get in the van," Jameson shouted. "Don't take nothin', just everyone get in the van and be ready to haul ass."

Frankie turned to go, but his father grabbed his shirt collar and pulled him back. "Get my shotgun," he whispered in his son's ear. Frankie froze. "Go, boy!" He gave his son a hard shove between the shoulders.

Frankie ran to the truck and climbed into the passenger seat. He locked both doors and cranked the windows up. He waited there in the cab, breathing heavily, rubbing his clammy hands on the legs of his trousers. When he'd worked up the nerve to take a look in the side mirror, he saw his father limping hurriedly toward the truck, silhouetted by rising flames which had fully engulfed the bally stage and tent.

Frankie crawled over and unlocked the driver's side door. Jameson hurried into his seat holding his side and cursing. He turned over the engine and took off as fast as the big truck could manage. He mumbled something, then shot Frankie a look of unrepressed disgust. Frankie turned away quickly, choosing to stare into his side mirror until they were back on the main road with no headlights visible behind them other than the van's.

"What the hell you gonna do now?" his father asked himself. "Ev'rything. Gone. Up in flames." He let out a maniacal laugh. "Nothin' left of the show but vehicles with nothin' to haul." He scoffed. "That kid..." He paused and put the bottle to his mouth. "Aw... T'hell with 'im. He gimme the damn...*willies* anyhow." Jameson's speech was slurred. He secured the bottle between his legs, then examined his right hand, opening and closing his fist, fluttering his fingers.

When Frankie began to nod off, Jameson slapped the back of his head. "Wake up, 'fore you fall into the flurburd." Frankie glanced at his father, whose lids were hanging heavy over his eyes. He watched him take another pull from the bottle, then he drifted off again.

Frankie awakened as momentum from a sharp left turn tossed him against the passenger door.

"Thss road's like a...a damned carn...vul ride," he heard his father mutter. "Turnin' this way, 'n thataway, this way, 'n thataway, this..."

Frankie jerked awake again with the GMC listing to the right, the tires screeching.

"'N turnin', 'n turnin'... Thisss fuckin' waaay, 'n thaaat fuckin' waaay..."

Frankie fought to stay awake but again succumbed to slumber. "Come with me, Frankie," a voice commanded. A shape began to form, eclipsing a brilliant whiteness. As it drew nearer, Frankie gazed into eyes that shone like sapphire gemstones. "You'll be okay, Frankie. You just need to come with me. Now," the voice urged. Frankie stepped toward the shape. He heard what sounded like the fluttering of wings just before he jolted awake.

The van skidded to a stop on the road above him. In the glow of its headlights, Frankie watched the towering trees topple like dominoes, the sharp cracking sounds of their trunks snapping in two. Finally, there came a low, sickening crash that reverberated within the mountains. Frankie struggled to his feet and took hold of a low-hanging branch to steady himself. His gaze followed the path of destruction to the twisted remains of his father's GMC truck and its crumpled trailer lying across the narrow fast-flowing river, its rerouted water gushing white around the enormous foreign objects.

"Oh God," he heard Lois scream. "Frankie boy. Oh God. Frankie!"

Lois and the twins rushed to the spot where the truck had gone over the bluff.

"Oh Jesus. No!" Jeb cried out. "We oughtn't to let Frankie go with him. Boss in the state he's in."

"We gotta get down there," Pokey said.

"Let's go, brother," Jeb agreed.

Before the twins could embark on their long and precarious descent, Frankie came climbing up the wooded embankment and into their sight. Their collective expressions of incredulity quickly transformed to those of relief.

• • •

The sun had just begun to top the mountain ranges and flood the valley with daylight. Frankie spotted Amos Tilley standing near the barn, a mug of coffee held at his chest. He was watching them approach, Frankie in the passenger seat of a black-and-white Myer County Sheriff's Department cruiser, the others trailing in the van.

"I appreciate the call, Josh," Amos said, as Deputy Joshua Prichard stepped out of the cruiser.

Prichard nodded, his expression grave. "Don't think any of 'em knew what to do or where to go. The boy finally pulled me aside and whispered your name."

"Frankie did?" Amos asked, his eyes narrowing.

"Yeah. I talked it over with the others, and they seemed willin' enough." Prichard slicked his hair back with his hand and worked his cap onto his head. He turned and yelled to Frankie, "C'mon out, boy," then motioned for the others to join them. The three emerged reticently from the van.

Amos glanced at Frankie and gave a half smile as the boy came to Prichard's side. "I'm so sorry about your daddy, Frankie."

Frankie nodded.

A pained grimace swept over Amos's face.

The others approached and clustered uncertainly behind the deputy. Amos smiled and nodded to them.

Prichard removed his cap and ran his fingers through his hair again. "You got any more of that coffee, Amos? Reckon we got plenty to talk over."

"Sure," Amos said, then motioned for Prichard to lead the way. To Frankie and the others, he said, "Let's all have a sit-down and get to know each other." He motioned for them to follow the deputy, and they all made for the house.

Inside, Amos served each of them coffee and Frankie a glass of cold milk. They took chairs at a long dining table adorned with pretty crocheted place mats. He scanned the faces, which were staring back at him blankly, then announced, "I'd like to extend an offer for you to stay here...till y'all find your way. You can stay in the bunkhouse at the back of the property. Used to be the milking barn, but it's been cleaned up to where it's plenty livable. 'Course I'll expect you to work here on the farm for your board and meals."

They each nodded, their expressions timid but agreeable.

"And you, Frankie, you're welcome to stay. To live here. You're a good boy, and I'd be glad to have you as family." Amos glanced at Prichard with a raised brow. "If we can work it out, Josh."

"Well, that's not my area," Prichard said, giving Frankie a quick smile, "but I bet there's a good chance it can happen."

"Only," Amos continued, shifting his eyes to Frankie, "if that's somethin' you think you would like, Frankie."

Frankie nodded, a suppressed grin evident.

Amos turned his attention to Jeb, Pokey, and Lois. "As you know, my name is Amos Tilley," he began, his tone a bit more solemn. "I've seen you come through over the years, goin' back to Frank Sr.'s sideshow days. Now I'd like to get to know you a little." He fixed his gaze on the Harpeth twins, with their yellow-white afros and pallid, freckled complexions.

"Oh, okay. I'm...my real name's Paul Harpeth. They call me Pokey," he began. "This is my twin brother, Jeb."

Jeb smiled, revealing short yellow teeth. "We're the ones what build the tip with our sweet, soulful harmonies. Then Pokey gets 'em roused with his spirited fiddlin'."

"This ain't no advertisement, Jeb," Pokey admonished.

Jeb lowered his head, then quickly raised it. "And I do some pretty fancy buck dancin'."

"Pokey and Jeb's got the purdiest singin' voices you ever heard," Lois added earnestly.

"That much I *did* know," Amos replied. "It's a pleasure

meetin' y'all. Lookin' forward to hearin' you boys sing some more. Perhaps some evening after you've cleaned up, you could come to the house and enjoy the RCA Victrola I have back there in the sittin' room."

"Thank ya," Pokey said.

"We...ah...can fix any kind of machinery," Jeb offered excitedly. "Can fix anything, really." He aimed a thumb at the kitchen window. "Kept that rust bucket goin' all these years."

"That's real good to hear," Amos said. "Seems like there's always something givin' out on me. I could use a couple of sets of hands that know their way 'round equipment."

Jeb nodded proudly. He turned to Lois sitting next to him and patted the top of her platinum mane. "This here's Lois McGhee," he said. "Little Lois. They call her that on account of how short she is."

Deputy Prichard snorted, earning a disapproving glance from the old farmer.

"She loves animals," Jeb continued unaffected.

"And animals love her back," Pokey affirmed. "Boss had a monkey once...that rascal hated ev'ryone but Lois."

"She knows over one thousand jokes," Jeb added with a trace of vicarious pride.

"They say laughter is good medicine," Amos noted. "It's very nice to meet you, Lois."

"Thank you," she squeaked, her round cheeks blushing.

"And Lois," Pokey continued, "she can make clothes and stitch cuts and do all kinds of other things of the sort."

"She can also be mean as a striped snake," Jeb added.

She gave Jeb's arm a hard smack. "You hush!"

"I don't believe that for a second, ma'am," Amos said affably.

"'Preciate your kindness, sir."

"My pleasure, Lois."

There was a moment of comfortable silence as they sipped their beverages and exchanged smiles. Finally, Amos turned to Prichard and asked, "You hear anything on the missin' Watkins boy?"

"Nothin'," the deputy replied with a shrug.

Frankie glanced at Lois and the twins. They conspicuously lowered their heads and remained silent.

"We tried to get the name and location of his parents...any relatives. Roscoe told us, far as he knew, the boy was homeless."

"Boy that age?" Amos said, his face twisted in disbelief.

"Yeah. And he struck me as a little closemouthed on the issue. Swore the boy'd just shown up outta nowhere at one of their revivals...up near Whitesburg. Tried to make it out like he was the boy's savior...givin' him a nice clean suit and warm meals. Takin' care of the orphan as commanded in scripture, he said." Prichard scoffed. "You ask me, Roscoe used the boy as a way of fillin' them white buckets he hauls 'round with him from town to town."

"Well, Josh, let's not jump to judgment," Amos cautioned.

"Aaanyway," Prichard said, "Roscoe said it ain't the first time the boy just up and disappeared only to show up somewhere down the road. Some of the others confirmed this. So I had to cut him loose. Couldn't very well hold a man in custody for takin' in a pint-sized vagabond, givin' him steady food, and puttin' clothes on his back." Deputy Prichard glanced through the window toward the road. "Reckon they've pitched their tent down the way by now."

"Hmm," Amos groaned, then drew a deep breath and let it out loudly. He turned to Lois and the twins. "How 'bout you have a look at the bunkhouse. There's two sleepin' quarters, not very private, I'm afraid. And you'll draw your water from the well right outside."

"Gotta beat sleepin' in the van," Jeb said.

"With you and your gassy—" Lois blurted out, then turned her head away in embarrassment.

"Fine," Amos said, suppressing his amusement. "We'll meet up later to discuss work chores and the like."

When they'd left the house, Amos turned to Frankie. "There's a nice room on the top floor I think you'll like. It was my son's bedroom. He enjoyed the view from out that window."

Frankie nodded.

"Good," Amos said, motioning him toward the main staircase. "I'm going to have a talk with Deputy Prichard. Then we'll get outside and enjoy this beautiful day."

• • •

That night, in his new bedroom on the top floor of Amos Tilley's handsome farmhouse, Frankie lay in the single bed, staring up at the ceiling planks. He tried to think good thoughts. Each time something sad or frightening entered his mind, he pushed it out and conjured up something pleasing to take its place. When the image of his mother came to him, leaning awkwardly against the wall of their narrow hallway, a dark stain growing on her white nightgown, he replaced it with that of her sitting opposite him, cross-legged on the linoleum kitchen floor, her long dress tucked under her knees, bouncing the little ball and laughing as she scooped up a coffee bean and caught the ball before it landed.

When the thought of Jarvis came to him, the gentle giant crushed beneath the weight of a massive bale of hay, Frankie remembered riding atop Jarvis's broad shoulders as he lumbered down the moonlit midway long after the shows had ended. The feel of Jarvis's huge protective hands clamped around his ankles as he proudly waved to the gawking carnies and stragglers. The image of Teddy Watkins came next: the soiled red handkerchief stuffed into the boy's mouth, the bright blue confident eyes smiling from behind the confines of the wire monkey cage. Frankie replaced it with an image of the boy rising off the pulpit floor, his eyes closed, praying for God to heal some poor soul. Just as Preston the printer had described.

Right before he dozed off, Frankie heard a whisper. "He hears you, Frankie. You'll be okay."

When Amos knocked on the bedroom door the next morning, Frankie was awake and standing by the window. With no verbal response, Amos slowly opened the door and peeked his head in. Frankie let go of the curtain and turned to face him.

"How'd you sleep in here, son?"

Frankie gave an affirmative nod.

"Good. Good. Lois and Pokey have offered to make us all a big breakfast. Everything fresh from the farm." He stepped into the room. "They say Jeb's still asleep and snorin' like a foghorn."

Frankie grinned knowingly.

"Think it's gonna be a pretty one," Amos said, stepping to the window. He pushed the curtains aside, leaned over, and scanned the vast field dotted with newly baled hay.

"Mr. Tilley?"

Amos stood motionless for a long moment. Then he slowly turned to face the boy who, at least to his ears, had not uttered a single word in over four years.

"Di... Did you..." Frankie's newly found voice broke.

"What's that, son?" Amos said, gently urging him on.

"Do you...remember Jarvis?" he managed to ask.

The old farmer knelt on one knee and put his arm around Frankie's waist. "Remember Jarvis?" He gave the boy a light squeeze, then returned his gaze to the window. "You bet I do, Frankie."

TEENAGE
LOVE

SHAWN LUSK HAD felt the shift in their relationship during those last few weeks. The first hint came on one of their many clandestine trips into rural Myer County. They were parked in his big work truck at their usual spot, a derelict boat launch on a secluded stretch of Lake Olivia's southernmost shore. As they kissed, her mouth remained motionless, her soft lips unresponsive. He opened his eyes to see Lisa staring blankly out the front windshield.

That was the first thing. It was a little thing, but it was something.

She'd accumulated a thick stack of acceptance letters from colleges and universities. As their high school graduation loomed, Shawn's apprehension grew. He became clingy, possessive, almost desperate when discussing plans for their future.

As a graduation gift, his dad had helped him purchase an old lake cabin, which Shawn planned to renovate. He would try coaxing Lisa into moving in with him after graduation, hoping she might accept an offer from a regional school within commuting distance of Olivia. He'd asked her several times to come see his little fixer-upper; it never seemed to be a good time.

That had been thing two.

The night of their graduation, Shawn had reserved a room at a decent-looking mountain lodge just outside of Partonsburg. Lisa reluctantly agreed to the surreptitious night together. Shawn had prepared a pitcher of Tom Collins mix for the overnight rendezvous. They sat at the round table near the window overlooking the parking lot. Shawn drank four large plastic cupfuls. Lisa could not finish her third. He gazed at her expectantly, but she scarcely took her eyes off her cell phone. Eventually, they crawled on top of the bristly plaid bedspread. They kissed for a while, and Shawn began to grope. It went a little further than previously, perhaps because of the alcohol, but still not so far as to breach the pledge of purity she'd made during a father-daughter church function some years before. Until Lisa, who was never much of a drinker, stiff-armed him and hurried over to the little garbage can by the dresser. She began filling it with remnants of a personal pan pizza carried on a yellowish stream of cocktails. Shawn hurried over and tried to hold her hair away. He was too late.

Afterwards, while Lisa showered, he tied the open end of the plastic garbage bag into a knot and disposed of it in a dumpster sitting at the corner of the parking lot. Lisa came out of the steamy bathroom wrapped in a towel. She'd combed her wet hair back; her eyes were red and tired. Shawn sat at the table facing the window as she slipped into clean underwear and one of his "Lusk Decks and Docks" T-shirts. Then she virtually collapsed face-first onto one of the double beds.

Shawn stayed up and had another drink by the window. He heard a snorting noise and glanced over at Lisa. She whimpered, then drew one leg up and away from her body.

This caused her silky purple panties to reposition so that a good portion of a pale buttock was now showing against the back of her suntanned thigh. Shawn quietly approached with his phone and clicked one purposely framed photo as an unknowing Lisa lay on her stomach with her mouth half open.

He finished his drink, stripped to his underwear, and got into the other bed. Propped up by both pillows, he rolled his head to the side and concentrated on his beautiful half-naked girlfriend sprawled out across from him.

Lisa awoke in the morning complaining of an agonizing headache, her stomach muscles sore from heaving. Shawn hoped they would drive into Partonsburg and walk the main drag, maybe take the SkyLift up the mountain. Lisa promptly let him know that she was physically not up for running around the bustling resort town or sightseeing. They packed, and Shawn grudgingly loaded their bags and cooler in the rear seat of his F-250 for the ride back to Olivia. When he returned to the room, he found Lisa standing in the doorway holding up his iPhone, its screen filled with the last picture he would ever take of her.

That turned out to be the last and not-so-little thing.

Their breakup was quick, clean, and mostly uneventful. Lisa simply ceased all communication with him that summer after the motel incident. Shawn became withdrawn, interacting with few outside of his parents and fellow coworkers at his dad's company.

Lisa's folks were wealthy, but their only child was never spoiled. At Myer County High School, she'd studied diligently to earn her 4.0 GPA and had always held various summer jobs for gas and spending money. That summer after graduation, Lisa waitressed part time for the Brownlees at their Smoky Cove Tavern. Shawn began showing up during her evening shifts. He made a few woeful attempts at reconciliation. Unbeknownst to Shawn, Lisa had enrolled at a private college located in Middle Tennessee. When the end of August came, she was gone.

● ● ●

Nearly five years had passed when Shawn went into the kitchen one Sunday morning and saw a somewhat familiar face staring back at him. He snatched his father's newspaper off the island counter and stood there reading every word of the wedding announcement titled "Heartsted-Kelley." The last sentence read, "The wedding ceremony will take place on May 1 at the Lakefront First Baptist Church in the bride-to-be's hometown of Olivia. The couple will reside in Franklin."

After a wave of despondency had passed, Shawn studied the halftone image of the couple. Her makeup was heavy, he thought. And her hair, dyed white-blonde and cut off at the shoulders, was too straight. Too perfect. She'd gone sophisticated since moving to the big city to attend her uppity private college. He much preferred how she looked when she was with him. Hardly any makeup. A little eyeliner. Maybe some lip gloss. She was effortlessly beautiful, and her natural dirty-blonde hair flowed freely, except for the occasions when her best friend, Jill Hamilton, braided a section on either side and connected the two behind her head. He liked that look. He could see her pretty face better, the light freckles on her nose and cheeks, and the cute way she'd crinkle her brow when giving him that look that said, *Are you absolutely nuts?*

Lisa's fiancé, posed beside her wearing a big-toothed smile, had a prissy rich-boy look. His light-brown hair was slicked back, his nose slightly upturned, eyes bright, lashes long and feminine. Like Shawn, the groom-to-be worked at his father's company. Yet rather than slaving away under the relentless Dixie sun, Jonathon Kelley, with his advanced degrees and fated birthright, "had recently joined his father, Thomas, at the much-venerated Kelley Law Firm."

In the following days, Shawn, who avoided social media, reactivated his long-dormant Facebook account and spent some time during the lonely weeknights investigating Jonathon Kelley, his family's dynasty, as well as his high school sweetheart's more recent endeavors.

The workweek ended early the following Friday afternoon with Shawn having suffered a rare verbal admonishment from his father. He'd misaligned a section of deck he'd been charged with framing. Distraught, Shawn drove to the home he'd shared with his parents for the sum of his twenty-three years. He went straight to his bedroom, peeled the sweaty clothes from his body, and dropped them on the laundry room floor. He drank a couple of beers while he showered, shaved, and trimmed his mustache. Hoping to be gone before his father got home, he dressed quickly in cargo shorts and one of his assorted "Lusk Decks and Docks" T-shirts, then headed downtown to the Smoky Cove Tavern for a few more beers and a platter of fried food.

Shawn dined alone at a table overlooking the water. Bear Brownlee, who owned and operated the Smoky Cove Tavern and Marina with his wife, Erin, occupied his usual position behind the bar. Erin and their daughter, Bethany, took seats at a nearby table and began discussing preparations for Lisa and Jonathon's wedding dinner. From what Shawn could gather, it would be held in the private dining room with the subsequent afterparty taking place there in the tavern's bar. Shawn listened intently as the topic turned to Lisa's soon-to-be in-laws.

"They're *old* money," Bethany conveyed to her mother, unaware of eavesdropping Shawn gazing out the window with his back to the room. "Lisa told me all about his family's big house right off the downtown square. She said Franklin is a little like Olivia's historic district, but without the water. Just bigger and way more hoity-toity. Apparently, Jonathan's mother wanted to have the wedding at some historic mansion there in Franklin. She used her connections and had it all set. But Lisa demanded it be here in Olivia at her family's church."

"Now...I can understand that," Erin said in an empathizing drawl. "She spent practically every Sunday and Wednesday night of her life in that sanctuary. Plus, her granddaddy's in bad shape. He's not able to travel, bless his heart."

"Well," Bethany replied in a discriminating tone, "apparently Mrs. Kelley got all huffy about it. Lisa said her and Jon had their first real argument over where the wedding would be. Jon tried to convince her to at least tour the mansion for his mother's sake. But Lisa wouldn't budge.

"Apparently, it's not caused a rift in the relationship. Tomorrow night, for the bachelorette dinner party, Jon's mother has hired a stretch limo to take Lisa and all her friends and bridesmaids to downtown Nashville. There's a restaurant called the Mercantile Bistro; she rented them the private party room that takes up the entire top floor. It'll mostly be her friends from college. But her best friend Jill will be there, plus her crazy Aunt Mel and—"

Bethany caught Shawn's gawking reflection in the window. She scooted closer to her mother and continued the conversation in a hushed tone.

Shawn had heard all he needed to hear. He had a date and location. Just Lisa and her friends, with no Jonathan Kelley and his buddies, who, if social media pictures were to be believed, ran from nightspot to nightspot like a pack of booze-hungry wolves roaming Music City.

After finishing his dinner, Shawn took a stool at the bar. Bear side-eyed him, then filled a frosted mug with Miller Lite draft and set it in front of him. "You plannin' on comin' to Lisa's party?"

Shawn simply shrugged his shoulders as Bear hovered over him, wearing a black "Semper Fi" T-shirt and frayed USMC baseball cap. Things had cooled since their heated confrontation back in the summer before Lisa left for college. Lisa was waitressing there at the tavern. Shawn showed up hoping to talk to her. When she snubbed his attempts, he turned belligerent, necessitating an escort to the back door compliments of Bear Brownlee. Though known as a peaceful, perpetually laid-back friend to all, Bear Brownlee could produce an intimidating icy-blue stare. Those few who have been on the receiving end of that stare seemed quite willing to drop any issue they felt they might've had with the aging veteran.

Shawn glanced at Bear and shook his head.

"It's an open gig," Bear said. "I just don't want ya comin' in here startin' any of yer shit..."

"I ain't comin'," Shawn snapped. "Why the hell'd I want to?"

Bear grinned. "Okey dokey," he said. "You and yer daddy still working on the Worleys' dock?"

Shawn spent that night in his little cedar cabin. Over the years, its capable but dejected owner's renovation efforts had waned. Since being "rescued," its condition had actually worsened under his custody. Tools, assorted lengths of two-by-fours, and unopened boxes of tile earmarked for the kitchenette and the tiny bathroom lay strewn about the place. Several of its walls remained stripped to their studs in preparation for new electrical that would pass code. Dead mice, their necks broken under wire snap traps, lay in the corners of rooms and inside moldy cabinets in varying states of decomposition.

Befitting his mood, a heavy downpour came at around ten o'clock and lasted into the early morning hours. He drank months-old beer left in his fridge while sitting in the ratty recliner his dad had retired two years prior for a newer model.

There was no television in the cabin. No computer. No electronics of any kind but for his phone. The only sound was water dripping from the compromised roof into strategically placed Tupperware bowls borrowed from his mom. He stared at his own bare bloated stomach hanging over cutoff Myer County High School sweatpants. Then he recalled the tanned lean physique of Jonathon Kelley in the photos he'd viewed online.

He thought of those last desperate attempts to make things right at the tavern. Lisa, refusing to reciprocate, asking for his order as if he were any other customer, her head turned away.

Shawn drained his beer, crushed the can in his big hand, and tossed it onto the floor. He closed his eyes and gripped both armrests. After a while, his clenched jaws began to ache. He relaxed his hands and slowly raised the lids of his booze-soaked eyes. He worked his jaw around, creating loud pops on either side, then said aloud, "You *will* fuckin' look at me."

· · ·

Traffic began to slow as Shawn approached the overhead sign spanning the interstate. He kept straight toward I-24 West and I-40 West, which would take him to his destination in the heart of downtown Nashville. He would find parking somewhere close to the restaurant, which, he'd learned through its website, sat on the lower end of Broadway, the touristy thoroughfare flanked with restaurants, western stores, and honky-tonk bars.

It was the farthest Shawn Lusk had ventured outside his home county of Myer in the mountainous east end of the state. His father once sent him to a workshop hosted by a company launching its new boatlift product. That was just across the state line in North Carolina. And, of course, he'd spent time on family vacations and holiday weekends in the resort town of Partonsburg in the bordering county.

"You motherfucker!" The big SUV had cut in front of him from the "EXIT ONLY" right lane. Shawn laid on the horn.

His anger was deflected when an eighteen-wheeler passed by his open window. The torn sheet of newspaper floated off the passenger seat and fluttered around the cab of his truck. He caught it with his right hand and crammed it under his leg.

He passed an exit with a street name that caught his eye. He could not begin to pronounce the word, but it started with D-E-M-O-N.

Shawn screamed expletives while attempting to merge into the right lane after spotting the Broadway exit sign. His blinker proving ineffective, he swerved recklessly and took a few blasts from a horn for his trouble. Shawn stuck his arm out the window and gave a resolute gesture.

Broadway was crawling with traffic and pedestrians. The sluggish pace allowed Shawn to easily spot the Mercantile

Bistro on his right. It was a big three-story brick building with green signage and a ground-floor glass facade. A single spire crowned the historic-looking structure. Normally he'd not waste his hard-earned income in such a place.

The road dead-ended with the football stadium looming across the river. Shawn turned left in front of the Hard Rock Cafe heading north on Second Avenue. Then, not wanting to stray too far from Broadway, he took another quick left onto Commerce Street and was relieved to see a public parking garage on his right.

He pulled in, punched the illuminated button on the machine, took the ticket it spat out, and threw it onto his dashboard. A wall sign at the entrance read "$20 PER HOUR—2 HOUR MINIMUM."

"Forty fuckin' dollars," Shawn hissed. He quickly calmed, reminding himself that money was no longer a concern to him.

Shawn crept through the dark, cavernous garage filled with out-of-town vehicles until he found a spot wide enough to maneuver the big work truck into. Then he let the Ford idle, an AC vent aimed at his face.

Shawn grabbed his phone off the console and was about to shove it into his front pocket when he stopped and turned the screen toward his face. He began swiping through the endless photos he'd taken of Lisa during their intense relationship. He'd kept them all, both posed and candid. Lisa wearing her cute little visor during tennis practice. Several of her in the turquoise one-piece swimsuit aboard his dad's old Mako patrol boat—bought at a Myer County Sheriff's Department auction—while anchored in a secluded cove. Selfies of them together after the state championship game, the victorious Shawn red-cheeked and sweaty, Lisa smiling in her cheerleader skirt, her arms wrapped around his waist. Graduation day in their silky maroon gowns.

It was strange to see himself smiling. He was happy. She was happy too. *So, what the fuck happened?*

Shawn scoffed when he came to the next photo. It was the one from later that night. Graduation night. The one she'd insisted he delete. And he had, then later retrieved it from his iCloud account. Shawn pressed the side button of his phone; the curves of Lisa's exposed backside faded from the screen.

He closed his eyes and let his mind walk through the impending encounter. It came like scenes from a movie. Its setting had gained realistic detail after he visited the restaurant's website, browsing photos of the swanky interior of its ground-floor barroom. As he envisioned himself reciting the rehearsed dialogue, Shawn's hands constricted, the right with an iron grip on his iPhone, the left on the Ford's steering wheel. Then, with the verbal prologue completed, and an image of Lisa standing before him slack-jawed and dumbfounded, the scene reached its bloody climax as he took decisive action.

Shawn opened his mouth wide, releasing tension with each muted pop of shifting bones. The muscles in his face relaxed; white knuckles regained color. His heartbeat steadied, and his breathing returned to normal. He stuck the phone in his pocket and screwed his black baseball cap low on his head. He killed the engine and stepped down from the truck, landing heavily on the smooth concrete floor. The door lock horn alert echoed loudly behind him as he lumbered toward the elevator, the limp still evident from the nasty fall he'd taken on a jobsite.

Shawn noticed "Level 5" painted on the cinder-block wall as he approached the steel doors. He pushed the red button, then reached down and casually felt the outside of the bottom-right pocket of his cargo shorts.

When a small group came up behind him chattering loudly, Shawn left for the stairwell. The sickening smell of urine persuaded him to take the steps two at a time. Then, when he exited onto the sidewalk, a fragrant culinary scent wafted past him. Heading toward Second Avenue, he discovered the smell was coming from an Italian steak house on the corner. As he passed, he peeked in and saw a young couple sitting at a table for two by the window. He felt a fleeting and irrational annoyance toward Lisa. *That could have been us*, he thought. Then immediately doubted he would ever sit across from a pretty woman dressed up in nice clothes, enjoying an expensive meal, drinking red wine...

Navigating the crowded sidewalk along Second Avenue, Shawn tried to stay to the right, close to the buildings, a clearer path for his substantial girth. He noticed two young guys dressed like faux cowboys coming toward him. Both were bulky with muscle, the kind produced in a gym rather than acquired through hard physical labor. Their skin-tight T-shirts boasted elaborate designs, the front tails tucked inside dark jeans crowned with oversized belt buckles. Their cowboy boots clicked loudly against the pavement as they approached him. They walked side by side, taking up half the wide sidewalk, firmly aligned in Shawn's trajectory. He thought he saw one give him a quick glance and mouth something to the other.

Shawn lowered the bill of his hat, then stiffened his arms at his side, fists balled in anticipation. He kept his head down, watching his thick calves and sockless worn docksiders alternate into view. The cowboy's heavy shoulder knocked Shawn into a wide picture window. On the other side of the glass, members of a three-piece band turned with a start. The bass player made a silly face and said something to his bandmates. They shared a hardy laugh before turning their attention back to their audience inside the darkened bar.

Shawn felt a hand on his shoulder. "My bad, hoss," the cowboy-hatted one said sincerely. "I wasn't watchin'. You good?"

"Yeah," Shawn said.

"Hey, I ain't gonna lie," the cowboy said. "I was too busy starin' at the women. They don't grow 'em like this in Fentress County." He and his doppelganger shared a knowing laugh.

Shawn forced a smile. "No problem."

"All right, big man. Take care," the cowboy said, giving Shawn's shoulder a quick squeeze.

Shawn watched them swagger up the sidewalk, their heads turning in unison as two attractive young ladies passed them.

Shawn secured his skewed hat and rejoined the flow of bodies making their way toward Broadway. At the intersection, he waited with the other tourists until the word "WALK" flashed in white letters. Shawn crossed the street, then went right toward the restaurant. It was dusk, and the neon signs glowed against the facades of the old brick buildings. Shortly, he spotted the green Mercantile Bistro sign.

As he approached, a long white limousine veered into the ten-minute parking space outside the restaurant's entrance. Shawn ducked onto the side street adjacent to the building. He checked his watch: 7:47 p.m. "What the fuck?"

The bistro's front and a good part of both sides of its ground-floor barroom were comprised of tall black-framed windows. This allowed Shawn to keep sight of the Cadillac limo from his position on the side street. As he leered through the panes of glass, he caught a few suspicious glances from a table of diners. He shoved his hands into the pockets of his cargo shorts and began to scan the hectic surroundings as if just another wide-eyed tourist seeking out his next beer.

The chauffeur emerged, dressed in black from his little cap to his polished shoes. He hurried around and opened the back door for his passengers, offering a wide smile and a hand. The women emerged from the gleaming limousine like Hollywood elites arriving at an awards gala. As they huddled on the sidewalk, Shawn could see the top of a very blonde head amongst them.

"Fucking *move*," he whispered to those members of the party who were currently blocking his view of Lisa. A middle-aged couple glared at him as they passed by.

Suddenly, the girls broke from their cluster and began lining up alongside the limo for a group photo op. Shawn froze when Lisa came fully into view. It was Lisa, though not *his* Lisa. Corroborating the image in the newspaper photo, *his* Lisa had been replaced by this Barbie doll version with straight, silky white-blonde hair and a painted face. Her high school athlete's body had turned thin and angular. Her soft, youthful cuteness had aged into something more mature. *But you're still beautiful*, he thought, guessing she likely drew even more male attention with this glamourous model look.

He checked his watch again: 7:53 p.m. He'd learned the private third-floor space had been rented from seven to nine. His plan was to arrive while the dinner party was in progress. He'd wait in the bar downstairs, enjoy, he suspected, the best meal he would ever eat, while tossing down absurdly priced cocktails. It was to be a special occasion, after all. And as she exited through the barroom sometime after nine o'clock, he'd be waiting.

He checked his phone screen for confirmation: 7:55 p.m.

Inside, above the bar, a funky Art Deco wall clock showed 6:55 p.m. Then it came to him; he'd forgotten the one-hour time difference.

The white limo eased into the Broadway traffic, and Shawn's eyes followed Lisa and her party as they entered the bistro through the revolving doors. They filed through the barroom and out of sight.

Shawn stood there on the side street, pondering his next move. Inside the bistro, it was standing room only, with a line of folks waiting to order drinks at the bar. He decided to go somewhere to cool off, have a few beers, and kill some time.

Directly across Broadway was a bar with a neon sign flashing "The Cowboy Corner." Once again, Shawn moved with the crowd along a crosswalk. At the street-level entrance, he showed his ID and entered as a live band was covering Jamey Johnson's "In Color." The well-oiled crowd sang along to the sentimental tearjerker while one older couple swayed as one slowly near the stage. Shawn navigated the bodies loitering along the bar on his right. He spotted stairs leading to a less crowded second level and headed that way.

The upstairs area had its own bar. Shawn took a stool and ordered a beer. He scanned the walls, which displayed a variety of musical memorabilia, artifacts, mounted instruments, and album covers of mostly country artists. His phone vibrated in his front pocket. He retrieved it and checked the screen: "Dad."

He silenced the ringtone and set the phone on top of the bar as his beer arrived.

"It'll be four-fifty, hon," the bartender said. "Start ya a tab?"

She was a woman in her twenties with purple dyed hair, a bull ring in her nose, and arms swathed in vibrant ink.

"Uh...no," Shawn said. "I'll pay as I go." He pulled out his wallet and gave her a five. Shawn caught her eye roll as she snatched the bill from his fingers. The two repeated this exact exchange four times over the next forty-five minutes, with Shawn keeping an eye out for the return of the white limo through the front windows facing Broadway.

"Elvis is in the building," came an announcement from behind him.

Through a second-level side door came a short chunky man in late-Elvis attire, complete with white sequined jumpsuit, a long, scarlet-red ascot, dinner-plate-sized belt buckle, and a jet-black carefully coiffed mane above silver-framed mirrored sunglasses.

The impersonator strutted to the middle of the room and paused. In a deep squat, he wound his right arm a few times before freezing with the arm and extended finger aimed toward the bar. In an overstated accent, he announced, "The King needs to, ahhh...wet his beak." He snarled his upper lip and let out a chuckle. Shawn watched as flashes from camera phones flickered. A few bar patrons posed for selfies, and Elvis accepted their tips appreciatively. Then, with the handful of bills, he headed to the bar and took the empty stool next to Shawn.

"What'll it be, E?" the waitress asked solemnly.

"Ol' number seven, darlin'. Neat. The King is celebratin' tonight."

"And what's he celebratin'?" she asked gamely.

Elvis turned to Shawn as if it were his inquiry. "I just bought a clip of Elvis's hair. I ain't kiddin'. Come from a lady in West Nashville. Her and her husband run a little concrete company on Forty-First...out off Charlotte Avenue."

"I ain't from here," Shawn said flatly. He took a long pull

from his drink, then stared glibly at the rows of bottles along the back wall of the bar.

Elvis grabbed his arm, digging bejeweled fingers into Shawn's beefy bicep. "Paid two thousand dollars for it."

Shawn jerked his arm free and said, "You got took."

But Elvis insisted, "Nah. Uh-uh, brother. She had the paperwork to prove it. Won it after he went into the Army." He pulled a Ziploc bag from the pocket of his jumpsuit. "This is from the buzz he got when he enlisted in fifty-eight. The story is all there, 'bout the contest and the winner. That's her." He tapped a manicured nail on the black-and-white newspaper image of a young woman holding up a framed certificate of authenticity. "It's legit, brother."

"Cut the 'brother' shit," Shawn said, avoiding eye contact. "You lost? This ain't Memphis."

Just then, Shawn's phone lit up and vibrated. Again, the screen showed "Dad."

"Hey, bro—I'm just shootin' it with ya. You looked like you were down. Thought a visit from the King might cheer ya up." He pointed at Shawn's phone. "How 'bout a photo with E to send to Daddy?"

"I ain't payin' to—"

"Aw c'mon, man," Elvis said, shaking his head. "I don't ask for nothin' for the selfies. But if folks offer..."

"Right."

"Nah. I'm just here to celebrate—"

"Do it away from me." Shawn's arm lashed out before he realized what he was doing. His palm plunged deep into Elvis's ample midsection, forcing a loud exhale from the impersonator's open mouth. The front of his pompadour came loose and fell over his forehead. The silver-framed sunglasses slid to the tip of his nose.

"Hey!" the purple-haired bartender shouted. "None of that shit. Get yer ass up and on yer way. 'Fore I have someone throw you out."

Shawn grabbed his phone as he spun off the stool. He hurried out the side door Elvis had entered through. He went right, past a narrow alley, and stopped at the steps of the Ryman Auditorium. He knew of the place. His dad would reminisce about listening to the Grand Ole Opry on his parents' Zenith radio every Friday and Saturday night. "The Ryman was the real home of the Opry," he'd declared repeatedly.

Shawn's phone vibrated in his pocket. He lowered his big rear onto a step and checked the screen. His father had sent a flurry of poorly composed text messages.

"I know you upset. Call back."

And just how the fuck do you know that?

The next read, "Shawn Call so your mom don't worry."

Don't fuckin' worry about what?

He'd told his folks he was spending the weekend at his cabin, getting some work done on it at last. His father was especially glad to hear that bit of news.

The last text left Shawn puzzled: "Lisa made choice son. You should not be there. Please come home."

"How the *fuck* do you know...?" He fell silent when it hit him.

He sat there a long while, arms resting on his knees, his thighs pulled tight against his chest, holding his phone loosely with his fingertips as if it were a contaminated rag.

It was on his phone, as it was all company devices given to Lusk Decks and Docks employees—a locator feature ensuring his dad knew the whereabouts of his seven-member crew.

Just then, Shawn's ringtone sounded. It was his father. This time, he answered.

"Son. Son, what are you doin'?"

Shawn exhaled, "It's okay, Dad. I'm fine."

"Shawn. Wha—"

"Everything's fine."

"Why did you go there, son? Don't lie."

"I...I..." Shawn stammered, fighting back tears. Finally, he sniffled and wiped his nose with the back of his hand. "I don't know, Dad," he lied. "I don't know what I was thinkin'. I don't... I just felt like..."

"You can't trust your feelings right now, son. I'm holdin' your prescription bottle...right here in my hand. It's way off. You can't just stop this whenever you want. There's consequences. There's chemical...uh...effects... 'Member what Dr. Rosselli said?"

Rosselli also said he could no longer provide the exorbitant dosage of pain meds he'd allowed Shawn to grow dependent on. He'd slipped off the boat dock he was roofing and fractured his hip on a rock formation lurking just below the shallows. Months later, the good doctor had ceased his liberal script writing without explanation. Shawn decided to take the opportunity to cease his other meds as well. Cold turkey...across the board. After a period of hellish withdrawal, he began to feel as though he'd awakened from a long, medical-induced hibernation. That is, until the troubling revelations of Lisa's upcoming nuptials overloaded his newly exposed and vulnerable conscience.

"Yeah. I remember. I'm just... I'm fine now, Dad. You tell Mama. Tell her I'm fine. Okay?"

Shawn could hear his dad's muffled voice muttering.

"Okay, son. You come on home now. Right now. You just get in your truck, and you drive home. Hear?"

Shawn lifted his head toward the darkening sky. "Okay, Dad. Yep. Comin' home."

"Okay, son. Good. That's good. We'll help you sort through—"

"Dad. It's fine. I missed a few days. That's all. It's okay."

"We love you, son."

"Yeah. Love you too. Love Mama. Don't worry anymore. Y'all go watch your shows. I'm headed your way."

He could hear his dad's heavy breathing. Then his mother's muted voice.

"You're not too tired, are you? To drive home this late?"

"Nah. It's not even eight here."

His dad let out a reserved chuckle. "Yeah, time change. Shawn...you be safe. Pull over or...get a hotel room if you get tired. You hear?"

"I hear ya, Dad."

"So, we'll see you in, what...three hours?"

"'Bout that, yeah. See you soon."

"Okay. Bye, son."

"Bye, Dad." Shawn ended the call and laid the phone on the step beside him.

He sat there, uncertain, his eyes closed, head between his knees.

• • •

"Beauty and the Beast," they'd been branded back at Myer County High School. The quiet, stout lineman and the pretty, vibrant, ever-smiling cheerleader. Though the motto was bestowed teasingly, always in the back of Shawn's mind lurked the nagging notion that he somehow wasn't good enough for her.

His insecurities seemed confirmed when he escorted Lisa to the prom only to be left standing alone and humiliated as she took the stage to be crowned as one half of Mr. and Mrs. Myer County High School with Cameron Ridgeway, whom she'd gone out with several times before Shawn had started dating her.

Sitting there on the steps of the "Mother Church," he let himself imagine the union of Elizabeth Joy Heartsted and Jonathon Kelley, Esquire, now one week away. Half of Olivia would show up for the big post-ceremony blowout at the Smoky Cove Tavern. If not for this little trip, he would have likely watched from the back patio of his cabin just across the lake as the party spilled out onto the tavern's back deck. Having to listen to the hired band covering all the predictable tunes as the drunks danced and laughed and sang along. He'd been to a few of them himself.

After the big celebration, Shawn assumed they would spend their first night as man and wife at the nearby airport hotel, toasting themselves within the luxurious honeymoon suite. He envisioned Jonathon with a Cheshire cat's grin, removing Daddy Prude's purity ring from his new bride's manicured finger, placing it atop his tongue, and gulping it down with chilled champagne. The next day, as so eloquently revealed in the printed announcement, they would embark on an extravagant cruise of the Greek isles. Then, the newlyweds would return stateside to settle into their posh lives in downtown Franklin.

He then envisioned a future where he, Shawn Milford Lusk, sat alone in the weathered Adirondack chair on his deteriorating dock watching the rippled reflection of the moon on the surface of Lake Olivia. A beer in his big-knuck-led, calloused hand, exhausted after spending another long workday enhancing the dock of yet another rich asshole.

The color white flashed in Shawn's periphery, turning his attention to present business. He drew several deep breaths, then picked up his phone and gazed at his own face reflected in its screen. He stroked his mustache and pulled the bill of his hat down, then got to his feet and, quickly but calmly, headed toward the Mercantile Bistro.

Shawn approached a couple of the staff taking a smoke break in front of the restaurant. They were chatting with Lisa's chauffeur on the sidewalk. Shawn gave the men a nod, then asked the chauffeur, "You haulin' anyone famous?"

"Better," he replied, wide-eyed. "Beautiful young women doin' the bachelorette-night-out thing."

"Like to see that," Shawn said.

The chauffeur pushed up his sleeve and checked his watch. "Give it about an hour, partner. It'll be worth it; I assure you."

"I've been up there servin' them," one of the staff inter-jected. "Margaritas. One pitcher after another."

They shared a mischievous laugh. Shawn gave a quick half wave and headed toward the entrance.

He entered the ground-floor barroom through the revolv-ing doors and was greeted by noisy chatter and refreshingly cool air. "Hello. Do you have reservations with us?" The host-ess was a cute chubby young woman.

"No. But...can I eat in the bar?"

"Of course," she said, "Anywhere you can find a spot."

He noticed a man relinquishing his place at the far side of the long burnished bar. Shawn plodded across the black-and-white tile floor and seized the empty stool. There, he would have a clear view of Lisa and the others as they exited.

The bartender came over to him. "What can I get you?" Shawn sensed the guy was taking him in. *Fuck you,* he thought, suddenly feeling out of place in the swanky room.

He scanned the house cocktails listed on the little plastic standing menu. "How 'bout one of them Tennessee Manhattans?"

"Yeah, man," the bartender said. "Those are excellent. Start a tab for you?"

Disarmed, Shawn began digging for his wallet. "Hey...can I eat here too? At the bar?" He removed his credit union debit card and held it out.

"Absolutely," the bartender said, taking the card. "We don't offer our entire selection—"

"No problem," Shawn said. "I'll find somethin' that'll do me."

The bartender let out a chuckle. "I'll be right back with a menu."

"Thanks," Shawn said.

He was beginning to feel relaxed. Resolved. He settled into the comfortable padded stool and looked the place over. The walls bore exposed brick wrapped in bulky crown molding painted a glossy white. Antique-looking mirrors were scattered on the walls and ceiling. The nicest place he'd ever eaten was the Smoky Cove Tavern. This was something very different.

A special place for a special occasion.

Shawn's shrimp cocktail appetizer arrived as he drained his second Manhattan. His New York strip steak dinner, ordered rare, arrived as he emptied a fourth.

"How does everything look?" the bartender asked, setting the oval dinner plate on the bar.

"Looks good," Shawn said. "Smells *damn* good."

"Good." The bartender chuckled again. "Need any steak sauce?"

"Nah. No, thank you," Shawn said, unrolling his napkin.

"Would you like to cut into your steak? Make sure it's prepared—"

"Hell no. Looks just right. Can I get another one of these," Shawn asked, nodding at his glass, empty but for a few cherry stems floating in melted ice.

"Absolutely," the bartender said.

As Shawn fiddled with his napkin, the silverware slipped out and clattered onto the bar top. His fork ricocheted into the air and landed on the tile floor just behind his stool.

"Aw, shit. Shoot. Sorry," Shawn said lamely.

"Not a problem," the bartender said. "I'll get you another."

When he left to fetch a clean fork, Shawn slid off his stool to retrieve the stray. As he did, he spotted Elvis through the window striking another deep-squatted pose as a few pedestrians held out their phones. After a brief exchange of words, he turned and began strutting up the sidewalk toward the restaurant. Shawn let out an exhaustive breath, then turned and set the dirty utensil on the bar away from his plate. He settled back onto his stool.

A very tall man, in his late twenties perhaps, approached the bar and stood beside Shawn. He had dark shoulder-length wavy hair. The guy was muscular, in the way the two cowboys were that he'd run into on Second Avenue, but this guy was dressed in silk navy sweatpants and a fitted pink polo. When he smiled at Shawn, his teeth shone comically white against his artificially tanned complexion. With the flowing hair, the build, and the ridiculous glaring smile, he reminded Shawn of the paperback romance novels his mother used to read during her bubble baths. He set a duffle bag at his feet and waited to be served.

"How ya doin'?" he asked.

"Good," Shawn replied.

The bartender arrived and handed Shawn a clean fork. "Here you go, sir."

"Thank you," Shawn said and immediately cut into his steak.

"Thing's still breathin'," the tan guy said, staring down at the bleeding slab of meat.

The bartender cozily greeted the man with, "Hey, buddy. What'll it be?"

"Johnnie Walker neat, please, Mike," the man said. "Double."

"Comin' up. Start a tab?"

"No, I just need a good stiff one in me," he said, rolling his bulky shoulders.

Bartender Mike let out a chuckle, but his customer seemed oblivious. When Mike moved on, the tan guy put both hands on the rounded, polished edge of the bar top and leaned forward, his triceps bulging under the tight shirt.

Shawn got busy with his meal.

The bartender arrived with the man's whiskey. He accepted the cash and was told to keep the change. Mr. Harlequin cover model emptied the glass in two long gulps. "Time to make some serious dough," he said to no one in particular. He reached down and took the duffle by its handles, then strutted, chest out and chin up, through the bar and toward the staircase.

Three-quarters of an hour passed. Three additional Manhattans had also gone by, and Shawn was feeling the collective effects. The bartender came to take his plate, which was empty but for the remaining traces of bright-red blood. Just then, muscle man swaggered back into the bar and retook his standing position beside Shawn. "Same, Mike," he said, slapping a twenty onto the bar top.

"How'd it go?" the bartender asked, snatching up the bill with his free hand.

"Oh, man. There's some sweet ass up there. Bachelorette's a cute skinny blonde. Real shy about the whole thing. Her girlfriends had to help her get into it. After a few drinks, she thawed out a little."

"Yeah, I saw them come in," the bartender said. "Pretty girls."

"Crazy as hell too...couple of 'em."

The two men shared telling grins.

Shawn felt the familiar tightening in his chest, the warming of his face and ears, the setting of his jaw.

"After I was sure she was plenty juiced up," the stripper continued, "I kinda half joking let the bride-to-be know I was available if she wanted to get one in before she was officially...*claimed*."

Mike the bartender chuckled. "Any luck with that?" he asked, placing the twenty in the cash register.

"Hell no. She politely declined. But let me tell ya..." He leaned forward and lowered his voice. "They had her sittin' in a chair in the middle of the room, the others circled around her. I was all up in her face with it. Her cheeks got bright red. One of the others said, 'You might as well see what you're passin' up.'"

"Oh, *man*," the bartender said, shaking his head.

"Yeah."

Shawn looked up at the guy; he was nodding slowly, a rapt smirk on his chiseled face. Then he said, "So...the other chick walks right up to me, grabs the waistband of my thong, and her and the guest of honor took themselves a good, long look."

"No kidding," the bartender said, his eyes flitting around guardedly.

"Not at all. I mean, the really drunk friend was laughing and havin' a good old time. But Miss Bachelorette...she was really giving it a once over. Those pretty green eyes lit up...like she'd never seen a dick before. Swear to God...I started gettin' har—"

Shawn's punch caught the stripper under his chin and sent him stumbling backwards. He ended up flat on his back, his head thudding against the tile floor. He clambered to get to his feet, but Shawn sprang off the stool and slammed a knee into his chest, pinning him down. The guy raised his thick arms to try to protect his face from Shawn's thrashing fists.

Folks quickly backed away, giving plenty of space between themselves and the one-sided brawl. Shawn's assault ceased when an arm clamped around his neck and yanked him off the battered stripper. When the hold was released, Shawn spun around to see the Elvis impersonator crouched low in a fighting stance, his short fat hands set for combat.

Shawn charged at him, then felt himself soaring through the air. He landed hard on his side, his impaired hip taking the brunt of the fall. During the flip, his father's stainless-steel revolver escaped the pocket of his Dickies cargo shorts, sailed into the air, and came to a noticeable rest in the center of one of the black tiles of the checkered floor. Gasps came in unison along with several cries of "Gun!"

"Three-fifty-seven, Smith and Wesson. Six-twenty-seven model," the King announced. He gave a quick whistle. "Beautiful."

Shawn winced in pain as he struggled to his feet. He scanned the room: the terrified faces lining its perimeter, the attractive young woman dipping her napkin into a glass of ice water and dabbing the stripper's bloodied face, and short, squatty Elvis standing wide-legged, hands on his thighs, his gaze fixed admiringly on the revolver in the middle of the floor.

Shawn darted across the room, swept up the gun, and scurried to the exit. Nobody in the barroom seemed especially motivated to impede the departure of the lumbering wild-eyed drunk with a stainless-steel weapon gleaming in his hand.

"That's right. You don't want none of this, big boy," Elvis called out after him. He was breathing heavily, and several buttons on his outfit had come unsnapped, allowing his hairy paunch to spill over the belt buckle. "Brother, I *earned* my black belt!" he said, then smiled and nodded at the flummoxed faces of the barroom's patrons. At last, he stepped up to the bar and said to Mike, "What do ya say, brother. One on the house for the King?"

Shawn sprinted across Broadway in the direction of the parking garage. Horns blared, and drivers cursed at him through open windows. He ran by the honky-tonk he'd nearly been thrown out of earlier and passed the steps of the Ryman Auditorium. At Commerce Street, he raced to the garage and entered its reeking stairwell. He located his truck on level five, jumped in and maneuvered the tight, narrow turns until he reached the street level. At the exit, his trembling hand eventually worked the paper ticket into the scanner slot.

He searched his wallet for his debit card. "Fuck!" he bellowed, recalling having given it to bartender Mike for his tab.

Shawn hit the gas pedal, crashing through the closed arm gate, and exited right onto Commerce. After taking the first left, he caught the red light at the intersection of Broadway. Shawn pulled his hat low over his eyes and stared across the street at the Mercantile Bistro. Between the slow-moving cross traffic, he spotted Lisa and the others, now donning identical white cowboy hats, standing at the back of the limo handing boxes and bags to the chauffeur, who loaded them into the trunk. He closed the lid and waited for a vehicle to pass. Then he went around and entered through his driver's side door. The women waved to the limo as it pulled onto Broadway.

Shawn watched them make their way down the sidewalk for their night on the town. Lisa, the belle of the ball, performed an impromptu clogging dance with one hand holding the hat on her head. Her efforts earned hoots and yee-haws from four men in a topless Jeep idling along beside them.

When a horn blasted behind him, Shawn looked up at the green light, then screeched onto Broadway going the opposite direction of the ladies. In the heavy traffic, he concentrated on finding an I-40 East sign.

Past the airport, traffic thinned. His attention turned to his excited ex about to embark on a life filled with more than he could've ever hoped to provide her.

Who the fuck was I kiddin'? began his internal rant. *A termite-infested cabin with a clear view of her parents' fuckin' mansion across the lake? So she could remember how good life was in Old Town before she let herself get stuck with me?*

Shawn smiled incredulously, then smacked the side of his head with the heel of his hand. "Who the *fuck* were you kiddin'?"

His thoughts turned to his current dismal predicament.

There'll be a wedding now, he thought, then punched the roof of the truck's cab.

He tuned in to a country station and cranked up the volume to help him clear his mind. When he caught the Sonic logo on an exit sign, he canceled cruise control and veered onto the off-ramp. During the 2.3-mile drive, he thought about the diner in Olivia out near the high school. It stayed open late on Friday nights during football season. Players, cheerleaders, and spirited students would gather there to celebrate that night's inevitable victory. The place served huge slushie-type drinks in various flavors. Inevitably, a bottle would emerge from someone's jacket pocket or purse. Vodka, rum, whatever they'd been able to creep from their parents' stash. They'd all pass it around, spiking their fountain drinks. Lisa might take a few sips of his. Afterwards, when she'd hugged and cheek-kissed her friends goodbye, Shawn would drive her in his truck to the derelict boat launch. If he was lucky, she might let him reach under her shirt for a quick over-the-bra feel, but they mostly just made out, kissing while his jaw popped, and her mouth and nose turned red and sore from the friction of his mustache.

Lisa was naturally social, but Shawn most liked those times when it was just the two of them in his roomy truck by the lake. Listening to crickets. Kissing. Until, inevitably, she would pull away and settle back into the passenger seat. When his breathing had slowed and the aching in his groin eased, he'd ask her again to come see the little lakeside cabin. The one he was going to fix up real nice, and they could move into after graduation. Just the two of them...him and Lisa. *His* Lisa.

Shawn pulled into one of the parking slots and cut the engine. He ordered a cherry limeade and waited with the windows down. Then, with the jovial fifties music pouring through the outdoor speakers, it came to him freely and effortlessly. Next Saturday morning, the day of the wedding, he'd borrow his dad's boat to go "fishing." Drive it down to his cabin and tie up at his dock. During the 6:00 p.m. wedding—to which he'd obviously not been invited—he'd enjoy a few cold cans of Miller Lite sitting there on the dock in his foldout chair. Hell, he might even drop a line in...help him stay calm in case his nerves were sputtering.

Per the discussion between Erin and Bethany Brownlee, the dinner for close family would happen in the Russell Sumner Dining Room immediately following the ceremony...give or take, depending on photography and all that. He'd wait for the party to move out onto the tavern's back deck. Catch them just as they really start to celebrate.

He thought of Bear. "Don't want me startin' any of my shit? Sorry, big guy... I'm gonna start a boatload of shit."

Shawn watched it play out in his mind's eye. Idling across the cove. Cutting the engine and coasting into the marina's no-wake zone. Taking hold of the Mako's loudspeaker before the band had counted off its opener. Demanding Lisa's absolute, undivided attention. Announcing to her before all her lovely guests, "You wanted to get away from me? Find you a rich guy and run around with them plastic people? Thinkin' you've moved on from the poor fuck you dated in high school? Actin' like you don't even remember me? I got some news. You're *never* gonna forget me."

Slowly, deliberately revealing the revolver from behind his back, leveling the barrel, and touching the muzzle to his temple. Pausing only long enough to register her reaction, then squeezing the trigger, blowing a good part of his head into the water.

As she stares down in disbelief, Jonathan, if he's indeed a gentleman, will turn his new bride away, sparing her pretty green eyes the carnage, as turtles and carp slurp fragments of flesh and brain off the water's surface.

Shawn grinned. "Sorry, sweetie. No happily ever after for you. Not haulin' *that* around in your bleached head."

•••

In the early morning hours, as Shawn lay in bed awake, his phone vibrated on the bedside table. He checked the screen and saw that he'd been tagged in a Facebook post of Lisa's friend Jill. His first thought was one of surprise that she'd not blocked him or unfriended him after Lisa's and his breakup. When he tapped the notification, a montage of photos appeared on the screen. There was a short message about their bachelorette night out, along with several candid pictures taken that night inside and outside various locales along Broadway. The one he'd watched being taken of the girls in front of the limo was among them. Lisa looked beautiful in every shot. He paused on a close-up of her taken inside one of the live music venues, her green eyes smiling beneath the white straw cowboy hat. Shawn felt his heart begin to race.

The bachelorette photos ended and were followed by a few older pics that included Lisa during her high school years. Jill had captioned each with humorous phrasing and silly emojis. Shawn froze when he saw his face in one of the pictures. He was in the driver's seat of his first truck, smiling through the open window. He was taken aback by how different he looked just a few short years ago. His hazel eyes were more noticeable and his jawline more evident, the double chin absent. In the bed of the truck stood the entire Myer

County cheerleading squad dressed in their maroon-and-gray uniforms, each making comical faces at the camera. Jill's caption read:

> Parade celebrating state championship win our
> senior year. Some great times! There's Shawn.
> Always such a good sport. Putting up with us crazy
> chicks!

He swiped through the comments, several of which were from old friends and acquaintances. One in particular caught his eye. It had come from Lisa. He read it carefully. Then read it again.

He dropped the phone on the bed beside him and lay there, unmoving, trying to identify the feelings invading him. There was relief, without a doubt. Guilt was another. He even sensed a trace of the passion he'd felt during their days together. An emotion that had been stifled in his formerly overmedicated condition.

He allowed his thoughts to flow freely. Basking in the usual joyful memories. Friday nights. Players, students, and cheerleaders gathered at the fifty-yard line in celebration and prayer. Spiked slushies at the drive-in diner. A quick hallway kiss outside Lisa's classroom. FaceTiming late into the morning, with a teasing Lisa wearing little more than his old scrimmage jersey.

When the suicidal fantasy clawed its way into his mind, he tried to shake it loose. When it didn't consent, he grabbed his phone and pulled up the photo. He read Lisa's comment a third time.

So true…poor Shawn! It was bad enough he had to put up with me. He didn't need the rest of y'all's drama! He was a sweetie!

It was followed by a smiling emoji face with bright-red, heart-shaped eyes.

Shawn closed the app and placed the phone on his bedside table. He couldn't help but grin at the long-forsaken prescription bottle his dad had apparently placed there for his reconsideration. Beneath those items, pushed to the very back of the drawer, sat the loaded Smith & Wesson revolver.

A knock came on his bedroom door early that morning. Shawn rolled over. "Yeah?"

His father opened the door enough to poke his head in. "I heard you come in last night. Just wanted you to know we're glad you're back home safe and sound."

"Yeah, Dad. Me too," Shawn replied with a trace of a grin. He could smell the aroma of bacon wafting in from the hallway.

"Your mom's cookin' a big Sunday breakfast. It'll be ready in a few minutes."

Shawn rubbed his eyes. "Sounds good. Thanks."

His dad gave him a quick thumbs-up and began pulling the door closed.

"You can leave it open," Shawn said.

His father let go of the doorknob. "So…you okay, son?"

Shawn sat up. "Yeah, Dad." He squinted into the morning light pouring through the windows and said, "I'm gonna be."

BILLY BURKHART DRANK three late-morning beers, hoping to ease the clawing hangover from the previous night's excess. His younger sister, Emily, had flown home to Olivia from LA the day before to sit for an interview with a local news reporter. Billy and best friend Bethany Brownlee had picked her up at the airport and taken her to the Romanesque stone mansion which housed the local television station WETN. During the filming, they waited in a cozy lounge, looking through some of the magazines spread out on a long glass coffee table. When they'd gone through those, they played with their phones.

"Hey," Bethany said, turning her screen to Billy, "here's another snippet on the movie." She waved her phone at him and repeated, "Hey." Following his gaze to the semicircle driveway, she noticed the black Hummer easing up behind her white Wrangler.

Billy watched through the tall windows as Kurt Sexton walked between the vehicles and swaggered across the drive toward the entrance. The heavy front door creaked open, and Kurt flashed by the lounge's glass-paneled door.

"Your buddy, Kurt," Bethany said.

Billy scoffed with a grin, though his eyes bore raw animosity.

"What the hell is with you and him? And Emily?"

"I used to work out at his club."

"Yeah. And Emily started goin' with you a few months before she left for Nashville. So?"

"Yeah. She was lookin' to get fit for the big move. She was rockin' along. I got her to shed ten pounds. She had a little six-pack goin'. Got her arms toned…"

"Okay. Cut the infomercial."

"Then one day, big mistake, I introduced her to Kurt. I had warned her how he hops from one pretty young member to the next. But sure enough, next thing I know, Emily and Kurt have somethin' going. But it burned out fast. A lot of tension between them. She kind of dumped him. Practically the next day, Emily catches him gettin' cozy with a pretty thing at the dumbbell station. Turned out, this chick was an old friend of Emily's. I remember them runnin' around together way back as kids. One day, in front of the whole damn place, Em caused this huge fuckin' scene. Gave this chick some serious warnings about Kurt. I don't know what she said. I wasn't there. He ended up threatening her with a defamation lawsuit. Said she'd hurt his business or somethin'. Daddy overheard them in a pretty heated phone conversation. He grabbed the phone from her and went at Kurt pretty good. But it all cooled off after Em left for Nashville."

"Typical Emily," Bethany said. "She never spoke one word about Kurt Sexton to me."

"Not everybody blabs every fuckin' thing they know."

Bethany extended a finger to him. They went back to fiddling with their phones until Emily entered the lounge holding an unlit cigarette in her fingers.

"How'd it go, Miss Hollywood?" Bethany said. Then, noticing Emily's jittery demeanor, she asked, "Hey, you okay?"

"Yeah, fine," Emily said, waving them to her. "Let's go."

"One girl's amazing journey from the backwoods to Hollywood," Billy said in his best narrator's voice.

"Pretty much," Emily said, working a red Bic lighter.

He raised himself off the sofa. "When's it air?"

"Tomorrow," Emily said, moving toward the main entrance. "Seven. Eastern."

Bethany gave Billy a look. He shrugged.

They followed Emily out the front doors. Outside, Emily stopped long enough to light up, then she noticed the Hummer.

"Yeah," Billy said knowingly. "Let's haul ass."

Billy climbed in back, then pulled the passenger seat into position for his sister. Emily jumped in, slipped on her Ray-Ban Aviators, and flicked the Marlboro Light across the pavement.

Bethany got in and started the engine.

"What kind a shit they ask you?" Billy blurted.

"Tune in," Emily said.

Bethany turned to Emily and laid a hand on her knee. "Hey..." she began, then frowned. "Oh, great."

"What," Billy said, then spotted the bulky figure of Kurt Sexton approaching Emily's open window.

"Let me out, Em."

"No one's getting out," Bethany said.

Kurt feigned surprise when he recognized Emily in the passenger seat. "Lookie there. How ya doin', Emily? Or Lacy?" he said, then flashed a sardonic smile.

Emily stared ahead.

He glanced at Billy in the rear seat. "Hey, haven't seen you at the club in a while. I'll give you a free month if you wanna get back at it." Kurt gripped the window frame of the door, his triceps rippling underneath a tight black workout shirt.

"I'm good, Kurt," Billy said. "See you 'round."

Kurt scoffed, then checked his watch. "Yeah." He patted the door and took a step back. "They treatin' you good out there on the left coast?" he said to Emily. "I hear it can be pretty brutal. Startin' to hear a lot of shit about the director's couch and—"

"Take care, Kurtis," Bethany said. The Jeep's tires squealed as she accelerated out of the driveway.

"What's he doin' there?" Emily asked when they'd gotten on the road.

"I don't know," Bethany said. "Well, they run his stupid little Appalachian Lifters Club commercials. So, something to do with that..."

Emily took a deep breath and let it out. "Let's get drunk."

"Hell yeah," came concurrence from the back seat.

They went straight to the Smoky Cove Tavern for a long night of consumption.

Presently, Billy was beginning to think he would live to drink another day. Their dad had taken Emily to the airport to catch an early flight back to California. Later that evening, she was to attend some kind of premiere party for her latest and much-buzzed-about movie which began streaming that very night. He could only imagine poor Emily's condition as she soared over the country. Help from a few in-flight Bloody Marys, he presumed.

Knowing activity was the best morning-after medicine, Billy decided he'd get some lines in the water before heading over to pick up Bethany for the tavern's watch party. By 4:00 p.m., he was feeling no pain. His beer cooler was empty, and he'd reeled in several decent small mouths and a couple of plump catfish. Were he heading straight home, they would have made the trip. His favorite meal, aside from the tavern's bacon cheese fries, was fresh-caught bass, filleted and thrown on the grill with just a little butter and Goya seasoning. And he had no qualms about frying up, in his dad's secret batter recipe, the catfish pulled from the murky depths of the questionable waters—children, pregnant women, and nursing mothers be damned.

After storing the rods and securing his tackle, Billy got on his knees, leaned over the portside gunwale, cupped lake water into his hands, and poured it over his head and face. He did the same for his bare shoulders, chest, and underarms, hoping to rinse away the beer sweat and revitalize after several hours under an uncharacteristically warm October sun. Then, he took the helm of his dad's old KingFisher, fixed his Oakley knockoffs in position, and throttled forward toward Bethany's side of the lake.

Billy idled up to the small weathered dock and tied up to rusted cleats. He grabbed everything he needed from the boat and staggered up a narrow flagstone path. As he entered the open backyard, two young girls stood frozen at their swing set, watching him approach as if he were something out of a backwoods horror movie. He wore nothing but cutoff Levi's and a straw cowboy hat that partially obscured his face. In one hand, he carried a camouflage rucksack, the other held a giant animal skull by one spiraled black horn.

Billy squinted at the two perplexed youngsters, his vision hazy from bright sunlight and alcohol.

"Wrong house, Billy!" came a voice from behind him.

He turned to see Daniel Colson and his wife, Elizabeth, laughing in the cockpit of their gleaming Chaparral Cruiser on their way to the Smoky Cove Tavern for the big night. Standing in the bow were Bethany's boss, Jeffrey Higgs, DDS, and his boyfriend, Colin, both with large red cups raised in his direction. As Daniel hit the throttle, Jeffrey hollered, "Billy, you stay away from those little girls!"

The big boat roared away, its occupants' laughter carrying across the cove.

Billy turned back to the girls and said, "Uh...sorry, kiddos." He gave them a dumb smile, turned, and headed back down the path.

He eventually found Bethany's house a little further upstream, one of many nearly identical A-frames nestled within a heavily forested peninsula across the cove from historic downtown Olivia.

After recounting his misadventure, he offered Bethany a justifiable defense. "I ain't never come this way by water. You can barely see the damn houses for the trees. And every fuckin' house looks like the next one."

"Well, I'll be sure to have a neon sign made for the dock," Bethany said. She gestured expansively. "Bethy's Place."

"Guess that'll end up on my to-do list," Billy said.

"Mm-hmm," Bethany agreed. "And by the way, those girls who were innocently swinging in their backyard when the *Deliverance* extra came stomping out of the woods? Their daddy's a state trooper. He's known to be a bit protective of his darling little angels. Doubt he takes lightly to trespassing either. You're lucky you weren't shot."

Billy released a long sigh of relief. "Shit."

Billy had grown up with Bethany Brownlee, whose parents owned and operated Olivia's Smoky Cove Tavern and

Marina. She'd even babysat him and Emily, helping out their single-parent father, Aldie, a long-time friend of the Brownlees. Billy was five years younger and several inches shorter than Bethany. As adults, the two had settled into an easygoing platonic relationship, she being as headstrong and opinionated as Billy was laid-back and peaceable.

When Billy spat brown juice into the grass, Bethany threw her hands up. "Did you not get the pictures I sent you?"

"Oh yeah. Stages of metastatic mouth cancer," Billy recalled. "Subtle."

Ever since her transition from managing the primary care office of Dr. Andrew Rosselli, to that of Jeffrey Higgs's family dentistry, she'd been giving Billy an earful over his use of dipping tobacco.

"I don't want to hear no more of yer shit about it."

"Fine," Bethany snapped. "Yuck mouth."

"Good," Billy said conclusively. "Happy...new house. Or whatever." He raised the animal head into the air.

"You're giving it to *me*?" She let out a squeal and gave him a big hug. "Shoo...you stink."

Billy had slain the massive bighorn sheep during his and his father's annual hunting trip to Idaho.

"How do you get it like...this?" she asked, rubbing the smooth white surface admiringly.

"First thing, I hung it in a tree in the woods behind the house."

"Why did you hang it in a tree?"

"Let the critters pick it clean," he explained.

"Gross. Then what?"

Billy shrugged. "Just soaked it in bleach."

"Looks just like your other one."

"Yep. 'Cept this one's bigger," he bragged.

"Mr. Moose is gonna go over the fireplace."

"I'll hang it for you tomorrow," Billy said, "if you promise not to call it a moose again."

Bethany fetched a couple of beers, and they relaxed in two patio chairs. Directly across the water sat the Ambrose house, a big white Victorian nestled within a pine forest at the tip of a peninsula. The mansion was now home to Ambrose's daughter, Lena, and her husband Andrew Rosselli. Not only did Rosselli take over the late and beloved doctor's home, but he'd also taken over his father-in-law's family practice. Despite an inauspicious beginning, the darkly handsome Tampa Bay–area transplant had expanded the business by leaps and bounds. The joke around town was that this growth could be attributed to admiring soccer moms. That turned out to be only partly true.

"Too bad you gotta look at *that* every day," Billy said as they gazed across the cove. "And too bad Burkhart Construction helps keep him in his comfy lifestyle."

When Burkhart Construction changed health insurance providers to one accepted by Rosselli's practice, the doctor had added a few more to his abounding patient load.

"I should sink his fuckin' Cabo," Billy said.

"Yes," Bethany concurred enthusiastically. "He spends weekends alone on that boat cruising the lake, spying on girls through his binoculars. I heard two of 'em down near Moreland—and they were pretty young—actually filed a complaint against him. Said he came right into their little cove, stood on the bow, and made some verbal...invitations. 'Course nothin' came of it. He's such a friggin' creep. I am *so* glad I don't have to be around him anymore."

"Aww, hell," Billy drawled dismissively. "All this shit goin' on right now... It's gotten to where you can't even pinch an ass anymore without losin' everything you—"

"Oh, you..." Bethany said, giving his arm a hard slap. "You *shit*."

"Ow!" He checked his watch. "It's gettin' close to show-time. I need to use your shower."

"Yes, you do," Bethany agreed.

Billy's ringtone sounded. He worked his phone out of his pocket. "Em," he said, then tapped the screen.

"Hey, sis."

"Hey, Miss Hollywood," Bethany called out.

Billy listened, then said, "The tavern."

As he listened for another moment, his eyes began to narrow.

"I'm over at Bethy's new place. Gonna shower and head that way."

Another pause. "Bunch of us. Dad and Willard. Jeffrey and Colin, Daniel and Liz... They just went by Bethy's place in Daniel's boat. Already plenty loose, looked like."

He listened more, then said, "Erin's gonna play the movie in Russell's room. Bear's gotta have the game on in the bar—"

He was quiet again, then gave Bethany a confused look. "Well, it ain't like Olivia's churnin' out movie stars right and left." Bethany came and hovered over his shoulder. Billy said, "I'm puttin' you on speaker."

"Okay," came Emily's thin voice through the iPhone.

Bethany asked, "So, what's the scene there tonight?"

"Crazy," Emily replied flatly. "About to head over to Sophia's for her big party. She's the director. Most of the cast and producers will be there."

"Oh," Bethany said. "That'll be fun."

"I don't know if I'm ready for more fun. Had enough with

you guys last night." She paused, then said, "Billy. Go take your shower. I wanna talk to Bethany."

"'Bout what?"

"Just…girl talk. Bye."

"Well, excuse the fuck outta me, Ms. Jaymes."

"Go on, stinky," Bethany said. "Squeegee the glass when you're done. And don't you dare use my loofah on any part of your body."

"Squeegee?" Billy said.

"The glass doors."

"Oookay then." He grinned at Bethany. "Bye, sis. See ya up on the flat-screen."

Emily scoffed. "Bye, asshole. Love you."

"Love ya," Billy said. He handed the phone to Bethany and grabbed his rucksack. As he approached the sliding glass doors, he heard Bethany say, "Okay, it's just me."

Billy and Bethany idled into the marina around 6:30 p.m. Bethany had been unusually quiet on their short trip through the cove.

"You good?" Billy asked.

"Yeah. Why?"

"Nothin'," Billy said with a shrug.

He tied up along the section of dock designated for the tavern's boating patrons. As they made their way toward the steps leading up to the back patio, they nearly collided with Benjamin Miller, who was shuffling toward them, head down, laptop under an arm. He was predictably dressed in a short-sleeved Hawaiian shirt, cutoff shorts, and dingy slip-on boat sneakers.

"Wi-Fi time, Mr. Miller?" Bethany teased.

Miller's head jerked upwards. "Oh. Hello, Ms. Bethany.

Billy. Yes. A bit of online exploration is called for," he replied, a lingering trace of his native British accent evident.

Miller was a writer who lived aboard *Elsa*, his 1980s trawler, one of the few vessels of its size with a draft low enough to clear Lake Olivia's shallower waters. He'd written several volumes of nonfiction, including his own memoir focused on his early nautical adventures upon Lake Huron. He'd also written two short-story compilations of Southern Gothic fiction, though most local bibliophiles could easily identify the provincial events that served as foundations for his plots.

"Emily's movie premieres tonight," Billy told Miller. "Gonna play it in the dining room around eight or so. You're welcome to join us."

"Oh?" Miller replied. He seemed to think it over. "Well, I've never had much patience for the telly." He tapped his fingers on the laptop. "Just needing to get a bit of work done, and then back to *Elsa*. But I do appreciate the invite."

"Well, if you change your mind..." Bethany said, then gestured toward the stairs. "After you, sir."

They followed Miller up the steps to the tavern's patio. The football crowd had already begun to gather for the eight o'clock kickoff; the fifty-inch SkyVue outdoor television was tuned into the pregame show.

Inside, Aldie Burkhart and Willard Oakley, long-time Burkhart Construction employee and friend, sat at a table near the bar with Jeffrey, Colin, and the Colsons.

"Hell," Billy said, scanning their table crowded with beer mugs, two big round metal platters of empty oyster shells, and several half-eaten appetizer baskets. "Don't wait on us."

Benjamin Miller continued toward the bar.

"You got time to howdy with us, Mr. Miller," Willard said,

giving Aldie an obvious nudge with his elbow. "Bear's Wi-Fi ain't goin' nowhere."

This brought Miller to a halt. He spun around and replied, "You know me, Willard. In and out. Although I do cherish every moment spent in this roomful of booze-soddened delinquents."

This brought a chorus of laughter.

"Save us two stools," Bethany said, "if you don't mind us sitting with you."

Miller gave a slight bow, then turned and made his way to his regular stool at the end of the bar.

Jeffrey checked his watch and said to Bethany, "We passed your house over an hour ago. What took y'all so long?"

Bethany aimed a thumb at Billy, who answered, "Took a quick shower. But then, my squeegeeing didn't pass initial inspection."

Bethany rolled her eyes. "Well, I wanted your *funk* off my glass doors."

"It's 'bout to start," Billy said, motioning Bethany to follow him to the bar. "C'mon."

They took two stools by Miller. A bartending Bear Brownlee made his way over and addressed the author first. "Miiister Miller, your usual?"

"Yes, please." Miller set his laptop on the bar, opened it, and began tapping the keyboard.

Bear grinned at his daughter, then at Billy. "You two gonna show yer asses again tonight?"

"That's on Em," Billy declared. "Don't know what the hell was eatin' her. She was friggin'...possessed."

"She's prob'ly nervous as hell," Bear said. "This is a big damn deal. Beer?"

"Yep," Billy said.

"You too, darlin'?"

"Why not?" Bethany replied tentatively.

"Wanna split some cheese fries?" Billy asked her. "We need to grease our guts."

"Lovely," Bethany moaned. "Sure."

Bear leaned over the bar and gave his daughter a peck on the cheek. "Missed you at breakfast. Your mom made the damnedest spread."

"I know. Sorry. Slept in a little," Bethany said, then yawned.

Bear nodded knowingly, then glanced at Benjamin Miller. "I changed the passcode," he said, grinning at the author's pinched expression in the glare of his screen.

"Well now, that would have been a most valuable bit of intel," Miller said, then exhaled dramatically. "Might I trouble you?"

Bear arched his brow, to which Miller responded, "Might I have the new goddamned passcode?"

"Why sure. KHESANH68," Bear said. "No spaces. All caps. That's K-H—"

"No need for a spelling lesson. I may have mentioned I was an award-winning war correspondent for a modest-sized newspaper...back in my motherland."

Bear chuckled and gave Billy and Bethany a wink. He looked back at Miller. "The gift shop sold thirty-five books last weekend, Mr. Miller. You're welcome, you grouchy ol' bastard."

"Really?" Miller said, with an uncharacteristic show of pleasure.

"Yeah. There was one of them hot-rod car shows up in Partonsburg. We always get a bunch of 'em on their way there...and back. I'll put your compensation toward the use of my Wi-Fi. Please let me know if there is anything else I can do for you."

"Just my cocktail," Miller said, typing away. "And please mix it with a straw rather than your finger this go 'round."

Bear chuckled, his big belly bouncing under his Marine Corps T-shirt. "You got it, Hemingway."

"Well, what do you have for us tonight, Ms. Isaacs?" Billy said, eyeing the framed cork board hanging behind the bar.

Among the pictures of tavern staff, patrons, local business cards, and a flyer promoting the live music schedule for "Party on the Patio," there was a glossy photograph of Loren Isaacs posed with the remaining skeleton crew of Burkhart Construction employees. It was taken at the end of a long work-day. Owner Aldie Burkhart stood in the center next to flamboyantly dressed Isaacs. Flanking them on one side was Willard Oakley with his arm draped over the shoulders of a young Billy Burkhart. On the other was James Boone, stand-ing partly behind and half a foot shorter than the smiling tele-vision host.

Miller glanced up at the photograph and announced, "Oh yes. The Queen visits a leper colony. I have that same photo hanging in my quarters."

Bear dipped his finger into Miller's drink and gave it a good swirl before setting it on a coaster next to his laptop.

Loren Isaacs had worked for the WETN News team for over twenty-five years. She was a homegrown personality. Locals of a certain age remembered her having begun her career as a tenacious on-the-scene reporter. She'd worked her way up to weekend anchor and ultimately co-anchor of the six o'clock evening news. Her current endeavor, *Mountain Moments with Loren Isaacs*, had her hosting, writing, and producing her own thirty-minute program spotlighting regional history, events, attractions, businesses, and citizens.

Burkhart Construction, Billy's father's company, for whom he had worked since he was a senior at Myer County High School, had been featured over a decade earlier. The segment spotlighted the housing debacle and its effect on well-respected local business owner Aldie Burkhart. He'd gone deeply into debt in preparation for his take of a recent land development. The collapse had left the one hundred-plus lot subdivision with only a few structures standing in various stages of completion within a sea of red fill dirt. Aldie had plenty to say about the inner workings of his country's financial lending institutions.

"Look at Boone," Billy said, snorting.

Again, Benjamin Miller glanced up from his laptop.

Bear chuckled as he dried a clean glass with his towel. "Yeah, strange fuckin' bird. Poor guy. Hell, I didn't know he was still alive till I heard he was dead. Last time I seen him was that night...the LSU game, remember, Billy?"

"Oh yeah," Billy replied, "Boone was a ragin' Cajun."

"Hell, I might not've recognized him if he wasn't wearin' that grungy Burkhart Construction hat," Bear said. "And the eye. That crazy damn beard hid half his face."

"He was in bad shape then," Billy said. "Wheezin'. Couldn't hear what any of us was sayin.'" He looked at Bethany. "Then, your daddy, Mr. Subtle, asked Boone if he was givin' him the stink eye."

Bethany frowned at Bear and shook her head. "What *did* happen to his eye?"

"He was on one of our jobsites...workin' the table saw. Tile he was cuttin' shattered, threw pieces up into his face. He never called anyone for help. Drove himself thirty miles to Foothills Trauma Center."

"Left him with a bunch of pink scars and a milky blue eye that stayed half closed," Bear added.

"Daddy felt terrible. He gave Boone an extended leave with pay until workers' compensation processed his claim. Then, instead of gettin' the prosthetic, Daddy said he drank all the money up, then piddled for a while as a handyman."

"I can believe that," Bear said.

"When he saw me," Billy recalled with a smile, "he said, 'You growed up.'"

"A man of few words," Bear said. "I knew it was gonna be bad when I gave him a tall Beam and Coke and he gulped it down like it was tap water."

"Yep," Billy affirmed. "Then, when I asked if he remembered Emily? His little helper? Told him how she's an actor out in Hollywood. He just ignored me and asked if Bear was gonna show the game."

"What an ass," Bethany said.

"He kept sayin', 'Gimme another drink,'" Bear continued. "Being all hateful. I asked him how many he'd had before he got here. He shoved his empty glass at me. Started slappin' the top of the bar and yelled, 'Pour me another goddamn one of these.'"

"Your daddy finally said, 'Think you've had enough.' Then Boone went quiet and sat all slumped over for a while, not even watchin' the game. When he started to nod off, Bear got him a ride home."

"And that was the last time any of us saw James Boone," Bear said.

The interview of actress Lacy Jaymes took place in a brick-paved courtyard behind the TV station's headquarters. Unlike the mansion's imposing, carved-stone facade, the casual backyard sitting area was softened by well-placed palm plants and flowers flushed with white petals. The ladies lounged on deep-cushioned wicker couches under a white gazebo. Host Loren Isaacs sat dressed in her ornate trademark fashion, ankles crossed, reading over her notes. Facing her was Emily Burkhart as actress Lacy Jaymes. At half the age of her interviewer, she wore torn jeans, the sleeves of her plain white T-shirt rolled up, and a Myer County High School baseball hat. She had her legs crossed like a boy, anxiously fiddling with the tongue of her Stan Smith tennis shoe.

"We'll start with some light banter, then move into your role in the film," Isaacs said. "From there, we'll follow the script we've agreed on."

"Okay," Emily said, adding a quick smile. Then came a fleeting moment of panic, causing her to seriously reconsider the interview. She even uncrossed her legs and leaned forward to begin her exit, but then the show's director came up to them and spouted off something about their sitting positions. Emily took a deep breath and settled back onto the couch.

"Better, Shane?" Isaacs asked after readjusting herself.

"Yeah, that's good," the director said. "You too, Ms. Jaymes. A little more this way."

Emily shifted toward him and crossed her legs again.

He seemed about to say something but instead scratched the top of his head. "That's fine," he said, then returned to his place behind the camera.

"If either of us flub up, no worries," Isaacs whispered to Emily. "We just stop and do another take."

"Okay," Emily said, nodding.

"Everyone set?" Emily heard the director ask. Then, "Roll."

The tavern grew quiet as the flat-screen above the bar showed a scene with Lacy Jaymes acting in her first role, a made-for-television movie which aired on the Lifetime channel. Another clip was from the limited comedy series, the first of a three-project deal she'd signed with the MovieNite streaming app's production company. Loren Isaacs's dramatic voice provided the introduction, which ended with "For this episode of *Mountain Moments*, I sit down with Hollywood actress and Myer County native, Lacy Jaymes, to find out how this foothills tomboy became Hollywood's it-girl."

> ISAACS: "Well, I want to start out by saying"—the host gestured toward Emily with upturned palms—"besides the dyed hair, which I assume is a residual from your onscreen character, it appears you haven't let Hollywood change you."

> The ladies share a spontaneous laugh.

> JAYMES: Yeah, my flight was late. My brother and a friend picked me up at the airport, and there was no time to get dolled up. So, you get me straight off the plane.

> ISAACS: I love it. Love it. Well, let's start by reminding viewers of the big premiere. It will be available tonight, streaming on the MovieNite app. And it's called *Who Would Believe Me Now?*

> JAYMES: That's it.

ISAACS: You've appeared in many projects and received very positive reviews, but this role has a bit more...*weight*, I guess you might say, than anything you've done previously?

JAYMES: Yeah. I've been able to play some really interesting and quirky characters and worked with a lot of great actors and directors. But I seem to linger in the rom-com genre. Not downplaying that. But when my agent brought this script to me, I felt like...this is the one. You know? This is *the* character I was meant to play.

ISAACS: Right. I've been a movie fan from the time my parents took me to see *Annie*, more years ago than I'm willing to admit. But, looking back, Carol Burnett was just *made* for the role of Miss Hannigan. You're probably too young for that movie reference.

JAYMES: Oh, I've seen it. My dad has it on VHS.

ISAACS: Okay, so you understand where I'm going. Some actors have that one role that seems tailor-made for them. You had that gut feeling when you read this script?

JAYMES: I did. There are those roles when an actor thinks, "This one's for me. It's mine." And it was the first time where I thought...I knew it would draw out in me something I hadn't revealed yet.

ISAACS: And we'll be getting into that "something" more deeply later. But first... You've been played up as this tomboy from the foothills, growing up fishing with your brother, helping your father on construction sites from the time you were just a little girl. And we have pictures proving these are not fabrications.

The screen filled with a collage of faded photographs of a young Emily Burkhart: one on a jobsite with a tool belt weighted down with assorted tools and a white hard hat strapped on her head, one holding a stringer of catfish aboard her father's boat with a shirtless Billy making a goofy face behind her, another in her Little League softball uniform posed in batting stance, game-faced and ready to knock one over the fence.

"Four-twenty average her last season," Aldie called out. "She was a chip off the old block."

Willard slapped his back. "Easy, DiMaggio. You forget I was on your team back in the day?" He glanced at the others. "He could connect, sure 'nough. But as a pitcher, couldn't find the broad side of a barn."

"Not true," Aldie refuted.

"Shhh," Jeffrey said, pointing at the television.

JAYMES: Oh God. When I find out who gave you those...

ISAACS: I'm sworn to secrecy! So, what was it like going from the southern Appalachian foothills to the hills of Hollywood? Quite an adjustment, I suspect.

JAYMES: Well, I had a buffer, I guess you could say. I spent a few years in Nashville before moving to California. And Nashville had really grown by the time I stepped off the bus. So I got to feel the big-city life. Or at least, *bigger* city life.

ISAACS: That's right. Your father had dreams of a country music star in the family, I hear.

JAYMES: Oh yeah. That was *his* dream.

ISAACS: Was music something you felt you had the talent to make a go of?

JAYMES: I thought I had some decent pipes. But there's a ton of talent in that town. I came to realize that every waitress, hotel clerk—whatever—could sing me under the table. But, hey, I'm glad I went. I gave singing a shot. Made some demos. Did some modeling. And eventually made the connections that landed me in Hollywood. Plus, I'm not real outgoing. I'm reserved. You have to sell yourself more with that gig than with acting. Acting, you show up and audition. You get the part or you don't.

Between takes, Emily stood and pulled a pack of Marlboro Lights from the front pocket of her jeans. She held it up to Isaacs. "This okay?"

"Yeah," the director answered. "Just move over there some to keep the smoke off the set."

"I had musical aspirations too," Isaacs said, following Emily down a brick path and away from the gazebo.

"Yeah?" Emily said, lighting her cigarette.

"When I was young, I used to watch the Reed Sisters on the public access channel. Thursday nights."

"Don't think I've heard of them."

Isaacs scoffed. "No, you wouldn't know them. But your dad might. They were superstars to me. That was my first yearning, you could say. I wanted to be the platinum blonde sister." She ran her fingers through her close-cropped hair. "I even told my folks I wanted to change my name to Joan. She could sing, play guitar, and write songs."

Emily smiled and exhaled smoke into the air. "Me and my brother are both named after country singers. My dad came up with William Roger for my brother, Billy. That came from Hank Williams and Jimmie Rodgers. Loosely." She made a funny face. "And I'm Emily Lacy. Emily after Emmylou Harris. Again, loosely. Apparently, my mother wouldn't stand for her daughter being named Emmylou. And Lacy from Lacy J. Dalton."

"And where did Jaymes come from?"

"Someone in LA suggested it. Nothing notable behind that one. Just thought it flowed, I guess."

Both ladies fell silent. Emily could sense the moment building. She turned and studied the rear of the massive building. Then she glanced at Isaacs, who was staring at her with a sympathetic smile.

"Intimidating, isn't it?" Isaacs said.

Emily nodded.

During the commercial break, Bear replenished beverages, and Felicia, a long-time tavern employee, busily transported hot greasy food from the kitchen to awaiting tables. Erin Brownlee emerged from the Russell Sumner Dining Room where she and a few friends were watching the interview. She carried a tray of empty wine glasses and baskets with the remains of fresh bread and honey-butter spread.

"Fill 'er up," she told her husband, setting the tray on the bar.

"Yes, ma'am," Bear said. He began grabbing glasses two per hand off the tray and setting them in the big sink. "Whatta y'all think so far?"

"Oh, we love it," Erin said. "She's just...so calm and cool. And so naturally beautiful." Erin glanced over at Aldie. "What do you think, proud papa?" She gave him a wink.

"Well, it's all in the genes, ya know," he boasted.

Billy scoffed and pointed directly at his father. "Them genes..." he began, melted cheddar cheese dripping down his lip. He wiped his mouth and pointed at the television. "Didn't have a damn thing to do with *that* face." He jumped off the stool and headed for the men's room.

Jeffrey Higgs howled. "Those genes," the dentist said, pointing Aldie's way, "gave Emily her weak enamel, which was turning her teeth gray. But Uncle Jeffrey was able to remedy the issue, and that's why Hollywood actress Lacy Jaymes has that dazzling smile."

"My hero," Colin joked. He grabbed Jeffrey's big head with both hands and kissed his cheek.

Jeffrey smiled, showing off his own artificially whitened pearls. "You're welcome, Aldie."

"I'll thank you when the bills stop coming," Aldie replied.

"Woo-hoo," Willard hollered. "*Get* him, Boss."

"Hey," Jeffrey objected. "You got the friends-and-family discount, Mr. Burkhart."

"If that's how you treat your friends and family..."

Jeffrey howled again and sent Aldie a semi-concealed middle finger in response.

"Bear!" Aldie yelled toward the bar. "Jeffrey just gave me the finger."

"Strike one for Dr. Higgs," Bear announced to the entire room.

This brought a chorus of oohs and applause from those familiar with Bear's three-strike rule.

It was a simple mandate: "If I have to call your ass out three times on the same day, you're gone." Though only playfully threatened on his inner circle, he had on occasion employed the rule with foulmouthed out-of-towners and once with a local kid who kept showing up to harass his ex-girlfriend who was waitressing part-time at the tavern.

Bear went to a small chalkboard hanging behind the bar. He hastily wrote the initials *JH*, the chalk clicking loudly against the black slate. He added a single purposeful mark beside them. More laughter and applause.

The levity in the barroom was stifled with the arrival of Kurt Sexton and his buddy from the gym. Billy emerged from the men's room as they entered and followed their bulky, swaggering forms toward the bar. He stopped at the table and put a hand on his father's shoulder.

Willard Oakley whispered, "Easy does it, Aldie."

Aldie replied with a nearly imperceptible nod.

Billy squeezed his dad's shoulder and, doing his best to sound casual, said, "Don't give him a second look."

The duo set their gym bags on the wood-planked floor in front of the bar. Kurt took the stool next to Bethany, though there were three empty spots to her left. Billy retook his stool between her and Miller. He kept an eye on Kurt and his buddy through the mirror behind the bar.

"What can I get ya, boys?" Bear asked, conjuring up a pleasant tone. He dropped a cardboard coaster in front of each man.

"Two Lite drafts," Kurt said. "You showin' the game, hoss?"

Bear's pale-blue eyes seemed to darken at the sound of Kurt's chosen moniker for him. He let it go, as he always did. Though, in private conversation, he'd expressed a desire to bring forth his daddy's Winchester 1897 hidden underneath the bar and allow cocky Kurt a close look down the 30-inch barrel. *Call me hoss one more time.*

"I'll turn it over after the...when the game starts," Bear said. "It's on outside if you wanna catch the pregame shit."

The flat-screen over the bar filled with the image of Emily Burkhart sitting on a couch across from Loren Isaacs. The graphic banner at the bottom of the screen read, "Lacy Jaymes: From Foothills Tomboy to Tinseltown It-Girl."

"Lacy Jaymes. The one and only," Kurt said to his buddy. They shared a stifled laugh.

Kurt caught Billy's reflection in the mirror and held his gaze until his buddy inquired, "What's with the dark hair? Wasn't she blonde?"

Billy was now staring blatantly at the two. He watched Kurt lean into his friend and whisper something. The guy snorted in response.

Bear set two frosted mugs on the coasters in front of them. He cut his eyes at Billy, then said to Kurt, "Watch yer mouth. Or I can pour these in a travel cup for ya." He walked directly to the chalkboard, erased Jeffrey's initials, and scratched KS in their place. Returning, he rubbed his hands together, his cold blue eyes glowering at the two men.

"Now, hoss," Kurt said, his tone returning to its natural volume. "No harm meant. That was a...*qualified* observation."

Billy straightened on his stool.

Bear made another trip to the board, added a second line, and calmly returned the chalk to the aluminum shelf.

Bethany placed a hand on Billy's knee and whispered, "Let Daddy handle it."

Bear, wholly adept at keeping the peace after decades of barroom management, made the men a polite yet convincing offer. "How 'bout you two grab a table outside. I'll have Felicia bring you a pitcher on the house."

"Aren't we special, Brad my man," Kurt said. He picked up his mug and raised it to Bear. "Here's to you, hoss."

Bear returned an unblinking, piercing glare. Kurt held his gaze briefly, then waved his free hand submissively. "Let Flea know where to find us." The men stood and headed for the patio door, each with a gym bag in one hand and a mugful of foaming beer in the other. Kurt kicked the door open with his tennis shoe, and they exited the barroom.

Bear glanced at Billy, then met Aldie's gaze. The wise veteran shook his head and called out, "He ain't worth it, Aldie." He pointed to the flat-screen where the interview was in progress. "You watch your girl."

ISAACS: In the few interviews you've sat for, you've often...*gushed* really...about your family and friends in Olivia just down the road. Tell us about your hometown. What it's meant to you. How it shaped you.

JAYMES: I miss it. I miss the community, the sincerity of its people. My mom left us pretty much right after I was born. My dad's construction business kept him really busy and working late into the evenings...weekends. But we had friends and neighbors who filled in. I didn't realize I was missing that maternal presence in the house. At least not consciously. But I'm sure there are things about me that show themselves...

ISAACS: What do you think some of those things might be?

JAYMES: Well, most obviously, I've never been accused of being too girly.

ISAACS: That's not such a bad thing. It's a tough world out there. And it's only getting tougher.

JAYMES: Yeah. In that sense, it didn't hurt being raised by a construction-working father and good ol' country boy big brother.

ISAACS: Both of whom I assume got plenty of ink in your recently completed memoir.

JAYMES: Oh yeah. My dad has absolutely nothing to worry about. There's nothing bad I can say about him. My brother, though? Rotten thing. It's *all* in there!

ISAACS: Fair warning, huh?

JAYMES: That's right. No, no. I'm kidding. He's safe.

At the bar, Billy's head spun toward Bethany. "Memoir?"

"It's an autobi—"

"I know what it is, Bethy. You knew about it?"

"Watch the show," Bethany said flatly.

ISAACS: Let's talk about the new movie. Without giving too much away, as this interview airs just before the movie comes available for streaming...one might certainly say it's coming out at an interesting time. A lot has come to light since you signed on for the role.

JAYMES: Right. Yeah. There was no Me Too Movement when this project was green-lit. We aren't trying to ride any wave with this, not to make light of the movement and what it represents.

ISAACS: This was already in the works. And your desire to take on this role had nothing to do with the slew of allegations that have erupted over the last eighteen months or so.

JAYMES: That's right.

ISAACS: You took some criticism over an online comment you made a while back. Can you give some insight to that...whole thing?

JAYMES: Sure. First, I absolutely support and sympathize with anyone who has gone through such a horrific event as rape, sexual assault... My remarks came well before the Me Too Movement, and they were made in hopes of encouraging victims to come forward immediately rather than waiting months or years. Some haters just decided to dig up my old comments and twist them as though I were bashing or questioning the recent alleged victims.

ISAACS: I believe the intentions of your comments will not be in question by the end of this interview. And your book will obviously stop some of the finger-pointing.

JAYMES: Yes. I think my intentions will be better understood. But as I watched all this unfold, along with the rest of America, I felt my past comments were verified, actually. Many of the recent allegations were decades old. There may be no way to prove or verify facts on either side. Someone could be guilty as hell with no way to prove it, or statutes of limitation have passed. Or the person could be completely innocent, but as a result of this collective cry for vengeance, someone's career, family...reputation...is destroyed. At some point during all this, the public began to regard all alleged as guilty, and, yeah, that didn't seem right.

ISAACS: And as far as your remarks...we're talking about two separate issues here.

JAYMES: Oh yeah. Nobody cared to read the dates on my comments. They concerned child abuse rather than the question of consensual versus nonconsensual contact between adults. I've learned there is a growing trend of treating any opposing opinion as a crime worthy of... Well, I won't say what a few imaginative commenters felt I was deserving of. But that irrational...*craziness* is a whole other discussion.

ISAACS: As ludicrous as some rhetoric might have been, it still made it more difficult to convince the producers that you were the right pick for the role of Marie. Is that fair to say?

JAYMES: Sure. It didn't help my efforts. There was one holdout on the production team. They certainly didn't want the film's lead being some apparent "rapist sympathizer," as one commenter had labeled me.

ISAACS: But then you requested a private discussion with this one...producer? And the result of that discussion is what really cleared the way. After that meeting, you were in?

JAYMES: Yes. There was no hesitation after that. And they helped with some PR that cleared the air a little. By the time filming wrapped, something or someone else was trending.

ISAACS: And we'll dive into the substance of that discussion. But first, let's watch a clip from one of the trailers. The movie, again, is *Who Would Believe Me Now?* Can you set the stage for us?

JAYMES: Sure. The scene shows my character, the protagonist Marie Oran. She's a twenty-eight-year-old sixth grade schoolteacher. And on this day, Marie is walking her class to the gymnasium and...meets the newest addition to the school's faculty.

The scene begins with Mrs. Oran leading her class through a long hallway, its cinder-block walls decorated by a fluid, vibrantly painted aquatic mural. She turns back to them and says, "This is your new gym teacher's first day. Show him what a good group of kids you are. Be polite and make him feel welcome. Even for adults, it can be scary starting something new."

She faces forward again as they enter the open vestibule of the school's main entrance. Marie notices the man standing at the gym's propped-open double doors. He is dressed in gray coaching shorts, bright running shoes, and a school-branded T-shirt with a whistle dangling at his chest.

He offers Marie an expansive smile while extending his hand. "Mrs. Oran's sixth graders?"

"That's us," Marie says.

"Rob Hastings," he says. Then calls out to the children filing into the gymnasium, "Coach Hastings to the rest of you."

"Welcome aboard," Marie says meekly. "Maybe you can whip them into shape."

"Don't you worry," Hastings says. He reaches into his back pocket and retrieves a small, round paddle, its surface motif the likeness of a baseball, and its wooden handle covered with a white grip like that of a tennis racket's. He gives the paddle a quick spin in his hand. "For anyone who tries to quit on me."

The camera zooms in on Marie Oran's concerned expression.

The next scene is a flashback to Marie as a young girl, similar in age to her students. She is walking with her father through the parking lot of a health club. The building is an angular structure of stained wood and large dark windows.

Young Marie frowns as she scans the building's exterior. "I don't want to do this, Dad. I don't need to know how to swim."

He looks at her in disbelief.

"Well..." she says weakly.

"Hey, I've cut my workouts to two a week," her father says

with an edge. "But still, I can't just leave you at home for hours at a time. Besides, everyone should know how to—"

"Ugh! Why can't I just hang out in the lobby. I could do my homework."

"Marie..."

"I don't swim!" she cries.

"Neither did your mother," he says grimly, then blows out a breath. "End of discussion."

Marie scoffs.

As they enter the club, her father says, "The kid, your instructor, is a Phys-Ed major. He's working at the club on an internship, so he's about half the price of the others I checked."

Another scoff. "It's a guy?"

"Marie. Enough."

Standing outside the glass-enclosed pool area, a young man greets them with a smile. He's wearing a college tank-top, rubber sandals, and a pair of Adidas sweatpants.

The verbal discussion between her father and the swimming instructor fades as Marie stands, arms crossed, watching a small group of senior citizens performing aquatic exercises.

When she hears the instructor tell her dad, "Well, I won't let her quit on me," she looks back at them with an annoyed expression.

The two men shake hands, and Marie watches her father depart down the hallway toward the weight room.

"You ready to get started?" the young man asks, opening the door for her. "I'm Rob."

Marie nods and enters the steamy room.

He waves her over to a table, slips off his sandals and tank-top, and says, "You can leave your clothes and towel here."

Marie steps around to the opposite side of the table, turns

away, and begins stripping down to her one-piece swimsuit. When she turns back to Rob, he is standing with his hands on his hips, wearing tight white bikini trunks.

"Their hour's almost up," he says, nodding his head toward the pool where the gray-haired women are waving their arms in unison. His eyes make a quick move over Marie's body. "Then we'll have the pool to ourselves."

The next clip shows Marie's husband, Wayne, in the kitchen of their home snacking on cashews and drinking from a bottle of Stella Artois. His tie hangs loosely around his neck, and his suit jacket is draped over a dining room chair. Wayne glances up to see his wife descending the stairs wearing an oversized hoodie with thick socks bunched at the end of her bare legs. She smiles meekly as she moves through the living room toward the kitchen.

"I love when you wear my shirts," he says with a sly grin.

"Do you?" she replies blandly. She pauses a couple of feet from him and crosses her arms. "Okay if we order out?"

"Sure." He brushes the salt from his fingers and puts a hand on her upper thigh. As he slides the long hoodie over her hip, she lightly pushes it back down and says, "Open a bottle of wine."

"Now we're talkin'," he replies gamely. Then, for the first time, Wayne notices the distant look in Marie's red-rimmed eyes. He takes her hand in his and says, "Hey, what's with the pouty face? Did that Davis kid backtalk you again?" Wayne raises his free hand and clenches it into a fist. "'Cause I think I can take him."

Marie smiles and slowly shakes her head. Then apprehension floods her face.

The scene fades to black, and Loren Isaacs's somber face replaces Marie's.

ISAACS: You've agreed to share some very personal experiences...that had a tremendous impact on you. And, I assume, greatly influenced your decision to fight for this particular role.

JAYMES: Yes.

ISAACS: I don't know how much you feel you can reveal...

JAYMES: Well, I'll start with the fact that I recently discovered a friend of mine was a victim of sexual assault. But she didn't report it and had only recently even spoken of it.

ISAACS: After you discovered this had happened to your friend, you said you contacted her. The two of you had dinner?

JAYMES: Yes.

ISAACS: And during your talk, did she tell you why she chose not to report it?

JAYMES: She only said that she didn't know how to deal with it.

ISAACS: But sadly, she's now dealing with it every minute of every day...

JAYMES: Oh, sure. I heard it in her voice. Saw it in her eyes. And my heart was breaking for her and what she'd gone through. By herself. And, of course, my own guilt over not warning her.

IsAACS: Because...her attacker was someone you knew.

JAYMES: Yes. Very well, so I thought.

IsAACS: I've done interviews like this with similar context. I've shed many tears with my guests over the years. My private motto is "No one cries alone in my presence." Knowing what was to come, I offered you tissues, off camera. You refused them.

JAYMES: I don't expect to shed any tears. I wouldn't give him the pleasure. Not that he's watching...

IsAACS: And "he" is...?

JAYMES: The same man who assaulted my friend had assaulted me only months before.

Droning stock music began as the screen transitioned from a tight frame of Loren Isaacs's concerned countenance to a wide view of the two ladies sitting on their respective facing sofas, then faded to a commercial.

Those within earshot of the television's audio grew eerily quiet. At the bar, Billy looked at Bethany with something like amused disbelief.

"Hey," Bethany said, taking her glass, "grab your beer and let's go sit with your dad."

"The hell's goin' on?" Billy said with a trace of annoyance. "Just c'mon."

Billy glanced at Benjamin Miller. The writer grimaced, his face filling with deep creases.

Bethany and Billy slid off their stools. They dragged two

chairs up to the long table where Aldie and the others sat in bemused silence.

Willard made a grunting sound, then glanced at Billy, his brow furrowed, head tilted. Billy shrugged, slowly shaking his head.

Aldie asked his son, "You know anything 'bout—"

"Not a damn thing," Billy said, his eyes inspecting the room.

"You, Bethany?" Aldie said.

"Not...not until just before we came here," she admitted sheepishly.

Erin Brownlee came through the door of the Russell Sumner Dining Room. She hurried over and laid a comforting arm across Aldie's back.

Aldie looked at her, a man in shock. "Why didn't she tell me?" he wondered aloud, his chin trembling.

"I guess she just did, Aldie," Erin replied softly. "Maybe in the only way she knew how at this point."

"Bless her heart..." Willard said. Then, in a tone that belied the flippancy of his words, "But she should've done s'more thinkin' on that."

Billy turned to Bethany and asked, "What'd she say to you?"

Bethany shrugged, tears welling in her eyes.

He turned to Elizabeth Colson. "Was it someone in LA? Did she say anything when you were out there?"

Elizabeth had one hand pressed flat against her chest, her startled eyes fixed on Billy. "Not a thing, Billy. It was an overnight business trip, so we only had dinner together. And all she said about this interview was that she was dreading it. But she hates interviews, period. So I didn't think anything of it."

"Oh great," Bethany whispered, glancing toward the tavern's entrance.

Amid the collective anguish, Dr. Andrew Rosselli had arrived and was waiting with an elbow leaning on the unmanned hostess stand. His dark intense eyes swept over his gawking audience. He gave a slight nod toward their table. Aldie, his face as stagnant as etched stone, hesitantly reciprocated. Erin offered a meek smile. Billy blatantly glared at him. Bethany looked away.

Billy turned to Bethany, Rosselli's former employee. His eyes narrowed, as if straining to read her thoughts. Then his glare returned to the doctor.

Rosselli gave a slight roll of his eyes, then glanced at Bear, who was staring at him from behind the bar. The doctor began waving a credit card held between two fingers.

"Felicia," Bear hollered.

Felicia emerged from the kitchen. Bear pointed to Rosselli, who now stood with his arms crossed, feigning impatience. "He call in an order?"

"Yep, I'll gather it up," Felicia said, then hurried back into the kitchen.

The doctor was among the unlucky few who Bear had once ejected from the tavern. But over time, the banishment was relinquished, if not Bear's sour sentiments toward the man.

There'd been no three strikes for Andrew Rosselli. At the behest of Russell Sumner's live-in nephew, the doctor had helped keep the beloved Olivia native and award-winning songwriter—in whose memory the tavern's private dining room had been named—wasting away in an opiate-induced fog in a spare bedroom of his grand estate. In retaliation to her father's "unfair" treatment toward him, Rosselli had promptly relieved Bethany of her office management duties at his practice.

When the *Mountain Moments with Loren Isaacs* graphic emerged, all faces turned toward the flat-screen in grim expectation.

ISAACS: Before you agreed to this interview, you told me that your reason for coveting this role was immensely personal. You also told me you would not be naming names. Not during this interview, and not in your memoir, which we'll discuss a bit later.

JAYMES: No, I won't be giving his name. It was a long time ago. We were alone, no one else around to corroborate. I can't prove it happened. As I read the script for this movie, I realized the character and I not only share the same trauma, but we experienced the same reluctance. And for the same reason...that lingering fear of not being believed. The difference being, Marie has an opportunity and feels the responsibility after many years to do something about it. To make sure it doesn't happen to others. At least, not at the hands of this particular man. For me, I'll live with the guilt... There's nothing I can do now. The man is deceased. Calling him out would only hurt his family.

ISAACS: The guilt being...the guilt of remaining silent?

JAYMES: Of course. Silence that allowed a predator to go on and assault someone else. Wondering how many others... It's crippling, and I'll be living with it for the rest of my life. While reading this script, it all...surfaced. And at some point in the months that followed, I noticed I could actually breathe when I allowed myself to think back on it. I'd had some offers to pen my so-called Hollywood story, but it wasn't until the movie awakened in me this...*thing* that I'd kept locked up somewhere in the back of my mind, that I finally felt I had something of substance to write about.

ISAACS: If I asked you to sum up your message...your reason for agreeing to this interview? Obviously, you are not simply here promoting a movie and a book.

JAYMES: It would come down to this: The time to report something, to tell someone you trust, to scream it at the top of your lungs, if that's what it takes, is immediately. Right then! Not ten years, fifteen, twenty years later. If anything resonates with the girls, young women, or *anyone* watching this interview, or who may watch the movie or read my book, I hope it is that. There is a toll the physical aspect takes on you, of course. You don't want to add to that any emotional guilt.

ISAACS: I hope the same. God bless you. And I understand and respect your decision to not call this man by name. But you did, at one time, confront him. Alone. Years after the fact?

JAYMES: I did. And I didn't cry then either.

ISAACS: Did he offer an apology? When you were finally able to look him in the eye, was there any hint of remorse?

Emily scoffs, then gives an inward grin. Loren Isaacs cocks her head uncertainly.

JAYMES: Yes, I looked him in the eye.

ISAACS: And did he show—

JAYMES: He told me very casually that...if I go around telling stories, I might end up without a mother *and* a father. In so many words...

ISAACS: He threatened your family? Pure evil.

JAYMES: And he did it with a disgusting smile.

ISAACS: Can I ask how old you were at the time of the assault?

Emily hesitates, then closes her eyes.

ISAACS: Would you like a moment?

JAYMES: There was a picture you showed earlier. I was wearin' all my construction garb.

ISAACS: Yes.

JAYMES: My dad took that the morning it happened.

The photograph of young Emily Burkhart filled the screen. She is standing among the two-by-fours of a framed doorway, her light-blonde hair tucked into a white hard hat. She wears a blue tank-top from the Smoky Cove Tavern gift shop, frayed cut-off jeans, and Dickies construction boots. A fully stocked tool belt hangs around her budding hips, her smile filled with braces.

The TV screen went black, and Bear tossed the remote control onto a shelf behind the bar.

Felicia came out of the kitchen and entered the barroom. She glanced quizzically at the stunned faces as she delivered a brown paper bag to the hostess stand.

"Thank you," Rosselli said. He tapped the screen of his phone a few times, then casually dropped it in the pocket of his white drawstring dock pants. He took the bag, then paused and glanced around the muted barroom. "Did someone die?"

Kurt Sexton burst through the patio door. He ran a hand through his hair and wiped it on his shirt. "Can you pull the awning, hoss? We're gettin' a few sprinkles out here."

The death stare he received from the Vietnam veteran was as hard and chiseled as the gym owner's calves.

• • •

The director pulled his headphones off his ears. "Thank you, Ms. Jaymes," he said. "Thank you, everybody."

As the crew shuffled around the set, Emily stood, unclipped the microphone from the front of her T-shirt, and dropped it onto the couch cushion. She removed the pack of cigarettes from the front pocket of her jeans and tapped one free.

Loren Isaacs came to her with outstretched arms. "Thank you so much."

"Thank you, Ms. Isaacs," Emily said.

"Loren."

"Loren," Emily repeated with a smile.

"Woman to woman," Isaacs said, "whatever I can do through my show, my contacts, or just personally, you have my number. Please don't hesitate to call."

Emily turned and exchanged waves with the crew, then made her way quickly through the courtyard and into the rear entrance of the stone mansion. Ignoring the subtle glances from behind windows and open office doors, she rushed through the foyer flanked with framed photographs of the channel's venerated alumni. When she burst into the waiting room lounge, Bethany and Billy looked up from their phones.

"How'd it go, Miss Hollywood?" Bethany said.

• • •

It was a cool March evening, and they were inside *Elsa's* cabin sitting on the cushioned benches of her dinette. Two fresh cans of Coors Light, along with several empties, cluttered the small table between them. They were poring over passages and possible revisions to their collaborative manuscript.

Over the past year and a half, Benjamin Miller had corresponded cross-country with Emily Burkhart via encrypted email. During her frequent trips home, she'd spent a good bit of time aboard his old trawler for face-to-face discussions. Regrettably, Miller frequently had to push her for more than she seemed comfortable giving. And though Hollywood actress Lacy Jaymes would later assure a viewing audience that she would shed no tears, autobiographer Emily Burkhart had not been so resolute.

During his routine information harvesting for background material, he'd interviewed one of her childhood friends. Her name was Claire Hightower, and she would reveal to the writer far more than he'd expected.

"She told me you two were best friends for a while," Miller said, smiling sympathetically.

"Oh?" Emily hesitated before affirming the claim. "Well, yeah, we were. We were on softball teams together. I went boating a few times with her family. Typical stuff."

"She told me about something that happened the summer between your sixth and seventh grades."

Emily gazed at the writer's withered face, her pleading eyes sensing what was to come yet desperate to be proven wrong.

"You were not the only one, my lady." Miller's face could not mask his empathy. "There were others. And Claire was among them."

Emily covered her face with her hands. "Oh no. Fuck no."

"Like you, she never reported it. Never mentioned it." Miller reached across the table and grasped Emily's forearm. He gave it a squeeze, then released it.

Emily dropped her hands from her face and rubbed her palms on the legs of her jeans. She finished off her beer and set the empty can off to the side with the others.

"The Hightowers had a pool," she began, followed by a few deliberate breaths. "Yeah, we spent a lot of time there during summer break. It was like...kidney-shaped with a slide and a diving board. They had a pool house with a big TV and a kitchenette and bar. One day, Claire and I were lying on lounge chairs in our swimsuits. Claire's dad comes out of their house followed by a short older man. I hardly recognized him at first. He had a beard, and his hair was longer. The scars were mostly covered. But his eye...

"Mr. Hightower waved at us and kept walking toward the

pool house. Boone slowed and just…looked us over. He didn't speak. Just smiled at us with his nasty teeth.

"As soon as he turned away, Claire nudged my thigh and whispered, 'Oh, gross!'

"I asked Claire what he was doing there. She said something about retiling the floor in the pool house."

Miller nodded. "Apparently, Mr. Hightower had asked your dad if he knew anyone who could do some work around the house. Aldie gave him a name."

Emily's hands returned to her face. She said in a muted breaking voice, "I never told her about him…about what he'd done to me. Instead, I stopped going to her house. And we were never close again after that. When school started back, we just never…reconnected."

Emily ended that emotional evening standing at *Elsa's* stern, breathing fitfully, wrapped in the sympathetic liver-spotted arms of the so-called grouchy ol' bastard, her warm cheeks wet with tears.

• • •

Billy Burkhart returned home from the jobsite to discover a manila envelope inside his screen door. He headed straight to the kitchen, dropped the parcel on the table, and retrieved a beer from the refrigerator. He went into his bedroom, laid his wallet and phone on the dresser, and changed into Levi's and a black T-shirt with the image of Johnny Cash giving the bird. His ringtone sounded; the screen read, "Lacy Jaymes."

He'd irreverently changed her name in his phone contacts from "Sis" to her new Hollywood moniker after seeing the words "Introducing Lacy Jaymes" in the opening credits of her first movie. That had been only a few short years ago when their nearly daily correspondence flowed as easily and frivolously as that of two college buddies. But Billy hadn't spoken to Emily since the interview aired. There'd been a few brief and awkward text exchanges, with Billy eluding any mention of the interview's substance or his baby sister's well-reviewed performance in her new movie.

He stuffed his phone into his pocket and returned to the kitchen for another beer. He pulled the tab on the can, then grabbed the envelope off the table on his way to the living room. He set the beer can on the sofa table and fell back onto the couch.

He assumed the envelope contained the CD he'd recently purchased online. But looking it over, he saw no postage. It was completely unmarked and a good bit thicker than a CD case. He tore off the end and removed a hardback book. He felt the textured dust jacket with his thumb as he scanned the authors' names, Lacy Jaymes in a large font followed by "with Benjamin Miller" in smaller letters beneath. Then the innocuous title *Tomboy*. He noticed a folded piece of paper within the book's pages. The handwritten note read:

A word from the coauthor...

Hello Billy,

This particular volume is much less my handiwork than it is a love letter, and I its courier. The message, both sad and hopeful, is from a tough, talented, but tenderly human young woman to the men in her life whom she adores adamantly. Though it will not be easy reading, for sure, you will discover there is much more to admire in your baby sister than the skilled rigging of a fishing rod and Little League batting

*records. But this I'm sure you know. God bless you
and your family.*

*Your friend,
Benjamin Miller*

Billy was surprised to find himself laughing aloud as his sister's chip-on-the-shoulder attitude came through loud and clear from the book's opening paragraph. Further in, he became aware of her unique viewpoint as a girl navigating through her little world filled with men. For the first time in his life, he was made to consider the maternal void in Emily's life as she conveyed, with ironical sympathy rather than discontent, the inexpert counsel of her well-meaning male surrogates on various important life matters.

When he came to the scene involving her attack, he mentally braced himself. With a clenched jaw and a sinking stomach, he read the passage:

My dad and brother had gone off to the lumberyard. I wanted to stay and keep building the house. My naive mind always assumed the houses we worked on would be completed by the end of the workday, whether it be day one or month three of construction. The rest of the crew loaded into a van and headed for Burger King. That left me and him with our lunch boxes. We were eating sandwiches on the second floor, sitting on plywood covered in sawdust and clippings of electrical wire.

His hand came over my face. It felt very rough against my nose and chin. He pushed me down onto my back. Everything moved very slowly at first. Honestly, it was not what his hands were doing as much as it was the look in his eyes. That was what triggered my panic—fight or flight, I guess you'd call it. Then everything seemed to speed up. Just a flurry of movements, hands, legs, and the sound of tools clanking around us. I reached down and grabbed a short Phillips screwdriver. It took a second to get a good grip on the handle. When I did, I began stabbing wildly at his face. The last thrust, I felt it give, and the bottom of my fist hit against his orbital bones. It had gone into his left eye. He rolled off me and started flailing around on the floor and crying out. I remember thinking he didn't sound like a person, but more like a wild animal.

Once I was free from his weight, I crawled on all fours across the floor to distance myself from him. I got to my feet, ran down the stairway, and out the front of the house. A good way down the street, I hid behind a porta-potty standing at the curb. Crouched down, I remember the smell of fresh asphalt. Minutes later, his rusted maroon truck sped by. I hurried back to the house, and as I waited there, I remembered all my tools scattered upstairs. I ran up there and began picking them up off the floor and arranging them back onto my tool belt. I even found the screwdriver I'd rammed into his eye only minutes before.

Billy's heart sank as he imagined the terror, shock, and con-fusion his baby sister must have gone through, both during the assault and all the years that followed. Then he thought of how the very toughness, for which she'd always received such high praise, had likely enabled her to conceal the event all these years.

At the Smoky Cove Tavern, the Burkhart men sat at the bar bouncing their mercurial thoughts and feelings off Bear Brownlee.

"I can understand that she was so confused...scared of what *she'd* done, she wouldn't have known *what* to tell anyone," Aldie commiserated.

"Why, sure. She knew she'd really hurt him. Thought she'd be in trouble herself," Bear added.

"There was also the fact that everyone loved the fuckin' man," Billy said. "*She* loved him."

"Me too," Aldie admitted. "How the hell could I *not* see—"

"How the hell *could* you?" Bear interjected. "He was hard-working, honest. Nice guy."

Aldie shook his head. "And funny as a monkey."

"Sly fucker knew how to play the game," Bear said. "Keep people off his scent."

Billy nodded. "Seems that way."

"You should give her a call, Billy," Bear said.

"I know. I will. Just not sure what to say," Billy admitted. He noticed Bear giving a wink to someone behind him.

"Don't worry about what to say," came Bethany's voice in his ear. She wrapped her arms around him and laid her head on his shoulder. "Just listen, dumbass. Listen to your little sister."

• • •

"Thank you, honey," Marie says, taking a glass of Cabernet from him.

Wayne nods at her plate of pasta. "Eat. That's my great grandmother's recipe."

She smiles. "Is it, now?"

"On my father's side. Sicilian."

"Right," she says. "You hardly ever mention the Orans of Southern Italy."

"Yeah, they're pretty mobbed up, so..."

"Well. There you go..."

On the table between them, her cell phone vibrates. Wayne flips it screen-down as he fills his own glass. He raises it to her and says, "So, here's to confronting this head-on. You're very brave, Marie Oran. And I'm so proud of you."

"Don't be. I feel just as anxious now as twelve-year-old me did at the pool all those years ago. I just reread the write-up he got in our little staff bulletin. The son of a bitch had been teacher of the year at his prior school. Community awards..."

"I know," Wayne says, wiping her cheek with his thumb.

"For the last five years, he's coached girls' soccer in the rec league."

Wayne watches her push pasta around on her plate. She lifts a forkful of coiled spaghetti noodles to her mouth only to lower it again, untouched.

"I keep thinking," she says, raising her hands in the air, "why would anyone believe me?"

"Some won't," he says, fingering the stem of his wine glass. "Until other victims see your courage and follow suit. What he did to you in that pool? So...brazenly? That conduct was *not* an isolated instance. He'll keep doing it until someone takes a stand."

"I worry how people are going to react. Especially my dad. Our friends. Everyone at the school…"

"Don't," Wayne says resolutely. He scoots his chair close to hers and takes her hand in his. "I think you're going to be surprised. By those who love you, who *know* you. The whole community." He gives her hand a squeeze. "Give them the time and space they need to…work it through in their head. Their hearts. But *trust* them. Trust them with your truth."

Marie looks into her husband's kind eyes. She smiles and he smiles back. He lets go of her hand, his expression turning grave. "I need you to do one thing for me, please," he says.

"What?" she says, the sense of dread evident.

He points to her plate. "Eat."

Marie lets out a laugh, then takes her fork and hurriedly twirls its tongs into the noodles. She opens wide and stuffs an enormous portion into her mouth, slurping up the lone strand hanging from her chin. Moans of pleasure are emitted as she chews enthusiastically and swallows hard.

"Honey," she says with a frown, "how the hell do you screw up spaghetti?" She wipes marinara from her face with a napkin. "It's absolutely tasteless."

Wayne scoffs. Then in a feigned hurtful tone, he says, "Well, don't be shy…"

Marie grins. "I appreciate the gesture, but I'd say I deserve a little better than this." She taps a finger on her cell phone. "Make the call. Pepperoni and green olives for me."

THE SANDSTONE
CROSS

INSIDE THE MUSEUM, which had once served as the prison chapel, two mop-headed teenage boys stood opposite the old man at a glass-topped table. They were examining a collection of crudely constructed "Confiscated Weapons." One of the boys, considerably bulkier and a full foot taller than the other, seemed quite amused at the whole prison milieu. The man overheard him describe in gloating detail the punitive actions he would take upon any inmate who dared attempt to assault him sexually. His hypothetical account culminated with swift and absolute castration.

Tough talk, schoolboy, the man thought.

When the boys caught him staring, the man grinned sheepishly, then moved on.

He made his way to a long wall lined with plexiglass display panels. Each contained synopses of the penitentiary's historical data, significant events, or persons of note. The man learned the former penitentiary had acquired its nickname, the Sandstone Cross, in the late 1920s after the original all-wood structure received its hand-cut stone refacing and a new configuration resembling a Greek cross. He read of the long and bloody history that included battles over convict labor—for decades the inmates were forced to work the methane-filled mines cut into the surrounding mountains. There were also riveting accounts of standoffs involving prisoners taking guards hostage, high-profile escape attempts—all of which failed, as those able to scale the prison's wall were not so adept traversing the rugged mountains—and grisly accounts of the incessant inmate-on-inmate violence.

The man had been on his feet for over an hour. He hobbled to a bench which sat along the wall outside the restrooms. He eased himself down, then rubbed his sore knee with both hands, checking it for swelling. As he rested, watching folks browse the museum's myriad artifacts, he couldn't help wondering what had brought about his sudden curiosity of the old penitentiary over 160 miles from his home.

• • •

Inmate Charles Roy Buckley had arrived at the Sandstone Cross in April of 1937. He'd gone by Charlie on the outside. On the inside, he was facetiously referred to as Lucky Chuck, as his ostensible good luck had earned him a bed in the infirmary so often that he'd grown rather chummy with its head physician, Dr. Oliver Swann.

Many times, Charlie had awakened in a sickbed with no recollection as to the circumstances which placed him there. Yet, his often-egregious injuries, which mystified their beneficiary once he'd gained cognizance of them, certainly proved well deserving of medical attention. Only much later, during his sleep, would a few confounding evocations divulge themselves to him.

This latest stay in the ward would likely be his last. What

brought him there on a frigid day in February 1952 was not the result of a violent encounter with a fellow inmate. Nor had he been buried beneath the rubble inside one of the cavernous mines scattered throughout the surrounding mountains. It had begun with a serious case of pneumonia, which, Dr. Swann implied, had ravaged his infected lungs long paralyzed by toxins from the tar of unfiltered cigarettes. No one dared blame the coal dust he'd been forced to ingest for his nearly fifteen years of incarceration.

"There's nothing more we can do, Charles," Swann had informed him. "I'm afraid the damage you've done to yourself is quite severe. Irreversible."

Alas, Charles was no longer serving the remainder of his sentence but living out the brief balance of his tumultuous life.

"Charles." He faintly heard his name being called as he dreamed...

He and his poor oaf of a cellmate sit with their legs splayed on the concrete floor. He expertly shuffles the deck several times, then spreads the cards in a semicircle between them. With the last of his Chesterfields on the line, the cellmate studies the illustrated pinup girls on the backs of the cards as if his concentration might affect the results. At last, he carefully slides a card toward himself, closes his eyes, and flips it over.

"It's been lovely doing business with you," Charles announces.

His hulking cohabitant watches him incredulously as he swiftly collects the cards along with the man's last cigarette.

Charles awakens in the infirmary, his torso wrapped in bandages packed with ice bags.

"Charles."

He's back in the cell lying on the top bunk, supported by a three-by-six-foot slice of metallic Swiss cheese. Below him is the very man who'd administered his injuries. He ponders the pattern of two-inch holes, plenty wide enough for a long, pointed object to be thrust upwards and through his flimsy mattress. He's the new guy, a *fish*, but still discerning enough to know he must keep his loose mouth shut about the pummeling. You don't snitch on he who sleeps beneath you.

Standing over the stainless-steel toilet, he tries to relax his aching body so that his bladder will release its contents. When it comes, he winces at the stinging pain as a red stream fills the bowl.

Charles awakened with a start. Dr. Swann stood over him. He took a few rustling breaths. "Hey, Doc," he said, his voice weak and raspy.

"Figured you were having another bad one," the doctor said.

Charles lay with his upper body elevated by two pillows. His bed sat in the back corner of the sixteen-bed ward facing the swinging double doors. This placement he used to his advantage by seizing the staff's attention upon their entrance with colorful insults, trifling complaints, or, on occasion, salacious jailhouse gossip.

"How are you feeling today?" Swann asked.

"Same as I look, I 'spect," Charles replied flatly.

Since becoming ill, his beard had grown long and bushy,

yellowing at its center. His eyes had turned yellow as well. His long skeletal arms, one crawling with pink scars, rested atop the bed rails. His distended belly bulged beneath a thin white smock. On the wall above him, a large ceiling fan forced tepid air across the cavernous room.

Dr. Swann smiled down at his patient with a clipboard cradled in one arm. "You look just fine this evening, Charles."

"Mm-hmm," Charles groaned. He raised his left arm, the one with the scars. Like his other, it was secured to the bed rail but allotted a twelve-inch chain lead—a modest liberty he often used to indiscreetly excavate the spacious orifices of his nose, discarding the matter onto his smock. He aimed his long-nailed index finger toward the double doors and asked, "Who's the new kid I seen in there earlier? Pretty boy with the sissy way 'bout him."

"Charles," Dr. Swann admonished, then chuckled good-naturedly. "His name is Kelly. Kelly Chase. And you'll get to know him soon enough. He'll be bringing your meds in the morning."

"I don't wanna know him," Charles said. "I don't like his look. He's got a woman's eyes. And a girl's name. Don't like the way he smiles. Like how some of them fruits gawked at me when I first got thrown in this hellhole."

"Well, I have to make my rounds," Swann said. He stepped back and gestured toward the two rows of occupied beds. "It's a full house, unfortunately."

Charles's face went blank. He dropped his hand back onto the bed rail. "Go on, then."

"Hey," Swann said, "I'll be back around late morning. In the meantime, don't be rude to the new attendant. There isn't exactly a long line of qualified applicants eager to work here. Don't *you* scare him off."

Charles nodded imperceptibly.

"Father Ramey." Swann's tone had turned sympathetic. "He asked again if you wouldn't want to see him."

Charles coughed, then swallowed what had come up.

"Use your bowl, Charles. That's why it's there."

Charles fixed his eyes on the water-stained ceiling above him.

"There's no pressure, Charles," Swann assured. "He just wants to talk. Or listen, as would likely be the case with you."

Charles either missed or ignored the doctor's bedside humor. "I tol' ya, I got nothin' to say to him."

Swann sighed. "Many patients in your condition...in your predicament...find it comforting to have a sympathetic ear, as it were. Talk through any regrets, any guilt—"

"I ain't got no guilt, Doc. Can't have guilt 'bout somethin' I don't remember doin.'"

Swann followed his patient's gaze to the ceiling. "But...you *did* do it, Charles."

Charles moaned.

Dr. Swann raised the clipboard and wrote something with his gold-plated fountain pen. He turned and walked to the next bed, the soles of his brown leather wingtip shoes clicking against the polished concrete floor.

● ● ●

Charles awoke restless the next morning. He barely touched his scrambled eggs and left the full cup of milk sitting on the little steel table by his bed. He stared overhead at the water stains until he spotted the new ward attendant, Kelly, standing at a rolling table arranging medications for the morning distribution.

He was dressed like the other orderlies, wearing a white short-sleeved button-down shirt with white trousers and a thin black belt. His black shoes were creased but well shined. Charles watched as he dropped pills into the small containers and filled plastic cups from a water pitcher. When Kelly was done, he threw a hand on his narrow hip, palm out, and studied the table's contents against the clipboard he held in the other. When the boy began pushing the cart his way, Charles moved his eyes back to the ceiling.

"Hello, Mr. Buckley," Kelly said in a soft, southern drawl.

Charles raised his chained hand and wiggled his fingers.

"My name is Kelly."

Charles made a snorting sound.

"I've got your medicine ready for you." Kelly extended the container of pills. Charles took it with his chained hand and emptied it into his mouth. Kelly handed him the cup of water and took the empty pill container. Charles took a few gulps and handed back the cup.

"Good job, Mr.—"

"Don't 'good job' me, condescending little fairy pissant."

Kelly made quick work of being on his way.

Later, Charles lay quiet, his mood as sour as his bedsheets. An orderly entered through the double doors. Charles paid him little mind as he studied the ceiling's water stains for signs of expansion. Only when Dr. Swann, Kelly, and two other orderlies burst into the ward did Charles take notice. The men hurried down the center of the room to the bed in which Knuckles had lain still as a mannequin for the last four days.

Charles didn't know his real name. He'd worked laundry with the guy. Maybe a year back? It was hard to say, as time moves at an altogether different pace on the inside. Knuckles had been pleasant. Peaceful. Quietly serving out his seven-year stint until he could be reunited with his family back home in...St. Louis?

Somber expressions beheld poor Knuckles. Charles watched as Swann laid a hand on Kelly's shoulder, nodded, then scribbled something on his clipboard. The doctor glanced at the wall clock and wrote something more. Then Kelly Chase reverently covered Knuckles's gray face with the bedsheet and began rolling his lifeless body down the long corridor created by the two rows of beds. Kelly gave Charles a benign smile as he approached. The young man's eyes were wet with tears. He turned and pushed old Knuckles through the double doors, where his rendezvous with the meat wagon awaited.

"You'll get used to it, kid," came Charles's belated counsel.

He eased his head back onto the pillows and closed his eyes. The familiar clicking of Dr. Swann's wingtip shoes grew louder. "Hey, Doc?" Charles called. He opened his eyes and glanced at Swann.

"Yes," the doctor said, coming toward Charles's bed.

Charles took a few labored breaths. "I...ah..."

"What is it, Charles? As you see, I have some unfortunate business to attend to."

"I'd like a word with the chaplain."

"Really? Well, of course, Charles. Why the sudden—"

"Just tell Father Ramey to pay me a visit. Preferably while I'm still suckin' air."

"I'll let him know," Swann said.

• • •

"Charles?"

He could faintly hear his name being called.

"Charles." Again. Louder.

He enters a dimly lit hotel lobby. At the front counter, the clerk hands him a key to room 11. As he accepts the key, he notices dried blood smeared into his hairy forearm. He jerks his arm back, but the clerk seems not to have noticed.

He enters room 11 and locks the door behind him. He tosses the key on the top of the cheap table, then puts his boot on the edge of the bed and lifts the leg of his trousers. The familiar turquoise handle of his seven-inch hunting knife is missing from its sheath. Realizing he'd left it in one of the rooms of the house, he panics. He goes into the bathroom and scans its surfaces. He searches through the medicine cabinet. Empty. He slams the cabinet door, causing its mirrored facing to shatter. Shards of glass cascade onto the counter and into the sink.

"Charles?"

He picks up a long sliver of glass.

"Charles."

Someone is calling his name from the hallway. He closes and locks the bathroom door. Then he steps into the tub.

"Charles? You in there?"

Sitting upright in the mildew-smelling basin, he tries slashing at the soft underside of his forearm. But no matter his intentions, his efforts are hindered. He leaves the bathroom, his arm bleeding from the superficial flesh wounds.

"Charles. Can you wake up for me?"

A naked woman lies beside him on the lumpy hotel mattress. He is undressed as well but for his bloodstained shirt wrapped around his arm. The woman stretches. Moans. Presses her body against his. Intertwines their legs. She inserts her fingers into his mouth. He tastes tobacco. As her hand plunges deeper toward the back of his throat, he gasps for air.

"Charles."

Charles awakened with a start, coughing, his head jerking about.

"Clear it out," Swann said. "Here, use this." The doctor leaned across him and took the steel emesis basin. He positioned it under Charles's mouth just as a glob of mucous and bile spilled out.

"I was afraid we were losing you," Swann said. "Be a shame for Father Ramey to have missed you by a matter of seconds."

"Huh?" Charles grunted.

"That must have been some nightmare you were having," Swann said, still holding the basin in his hands.

Charles's startled eyes flitted between the men standing over him.

"Douglas Ramey," the chaplain offered, eyeing the leather restraints around Charles's wrists. "Father Ramey, if that works for you. Or just plain ol' Douglas."

"Let me get you a chair, Father," Swann said. He walked

over to a rolling table sitting against the side wall. He set the basin on its lower shelf, then took the wooden chair next to it and carried it to Charles's bedside.

"Thank you, Doctor," Father Ramey said.

"Of course," Swann said. "Well, I'll let the two of you have your time."

Father Ramey watched Swann disappear through the double doors, then turned to Charles. "Mind if I sit?"

Charles shrugged and turned his gazed to the ceiling.

"I was given word to come see you. And swiftly at that."

"That so?"

"May the good Lord forgive my bluntness, but I'm told you are...in your final days."

"That's one hell of a bedside manner you got there, Father."

"Well, it's with that in mind I feel we've little time for idle chat."

Charles scoffed. "Speakin' of time. Bad timin' for you. I'm pretty sure I filled my rag during those last forty winks." He winced as he shifted in the bed. "You ever seen a grown man get his diaper traded out?"

"I don't think I've had the pleasure," Ramey replied gamely.

"It's a hell of a production. Takes four of 'em. Two of 'em to take each leg under the knee and lift my ass off the bed. Another works loose the muddied rag, rolls it into a ball, and tosses it into the haz bin. Then there's one more gets down there and really earns his nickel. He lifts my goose skin bag with his fingertips and wipes down no-man's-land. Now, if you're as fortunate as ol' Lucky Chuck here, you get the fella likes to inform everyone in the ward how small your bird is. Just for hoots."

Father Ramey nodded sympathetically.

"So, yeah," Charles said, "Let's hurry this along, 'less you wanna be here when the show starts."

"If you are being mistreated, I suggest you inform—"

"Oh hell..." Charles interrupted. "Reckon it's better here than back in the block."

Father Ramey produced a thick well-worn black leather Bible and set it on his knees. "A place filled with the incorrigibly wicked," he recited, his tone reverent. "Thieves. Murderers. The sexually immoral."

Charles wheezed out a laugh. "Yep, that pretty much describes us."

The chaplain tapped a finger on the Bible. "I was not referring to the prison population, Charles. Such are those—meaning those who refuse to repent and accept Jesus Christ as their savior—who will pay the penalty of eternal ruin. The second death, as the Book calls it. The lake of fire. The fiery pit. Hell. A big step down from even the likes of *this* place."

Charles gave the Bible a side-glance. "Should've knowed that thing would show up."

"You're hurtin' me, you damn fool!" The outburst came from the opposite end of the ward. Father Ramey turned in his chair. Charles peered across the room to where Kelly Chase was attempting to change a patient's soiled dressing.

"I'm sorry, sir," came Kelly's muted reply. "But it's got to be done. I'm trying not to hurt you, but it's gotta be cleaned and—"

"You not get no trainin' 'bout how to change a bandage without ripping the damn meat off the bone?" the inmate growled.

"I almost have it, Mr.—"

"Goddamnit, you done it *again*."

"I'm sorry. It's off now."

"When I'm able to get outta this bed, I'm gonna show you what pain is, boy." The bravado of this unveiled threat incited heckles from other inmates.

"Give him a chin check."

"Slice him up, Scottie."

"Nah," another protested. "Keep him in one piece for me. He's the closest thing to a broad I've seen in twelve years."

Encouraged by his ward mates, the man let forth a slew of insults at his flustered young caregiver.

Kelly pleaded, "Mr. Latham, I need you to be still while I—"

Dr. Swann emerged from the double doors followed by one half of the diaper team. The ward quickly fell quiet but for the *click-click, click-click* of Dr. Swann's wingtips.

With the ruckus temporarily quelled, Father Ramey turned back to Charles, who was resting on his pillows, his eyes stirring beneath closed lids. A long moment passed before the chaplain whispered, "You still with me, Charles?"

Wrinkles formed around Charles's closed eyes. His cheeks slowly rose as a grin crept onto his face. He rolled his head toward the chaplain and opened his eyes, his gaze steady and direct. "Where on earth would I have gone?" he asked suggestively. "Is this where I'm to confess all my sins, Father?"

"You need only to accept the Lord Jesus as the savior of your soul," Ramey replied unequivocally. "It is he who forgives the sins of man."

"Of course. You're just an old sinner, same as I." Charles gave the chaplain a wink.

"I am," Ramey admitted hesitantly. "Headed for hell, without doubt. But for the shed blood of Christ on the cross."

"The cross!" Charles spat. "Here a cross, there a cross... Around your neck. The very contour of this lovely, chiseled edifice. My mother had a cross. Wooden thing with a silver Jesus figure stuck to it. Hung on the wall just above her oft shared bed."

"That so?" Father Ramey said. "Let's talk about her...your mother. Was she religious?"

Charles eyed the chaplain. "Haven't bothered to peruse my psychobiography?"

Ramey studied him for a moment. At last, he opened his Bible.

Charles shuddered slightly, rattling the chain attached to his left wrist.

"Are you okay, Charles?"

Charles drew a deep breath through his nose. "Just a chill," he said flippantly, then drummed his fingers on the bed rail.

"Would you like me to ask for a blanket?"

"No need."

Ramey hesitated. "Well," he said finally, "let's waste no more time." He flattened the opened pages with the palm of his hand. "It is my belief that your spirit will continue on after this earthly life in one of two places. I would like to lead you to repentance. To bring you before God, cleansed of your sins so that you may spend eternity with your creator, Jesus Christ."

"Cleansed?" Charles repeated mockingly. "I'm sure I could do with a good cleansing. The aroma wafting from my nethers are testament to that."

Father Ramey observed Charles with a look of perplexity fixed on his gaunt face.

"Seriously, though," Charles said. "What better locality for a proper spiritual cleansing than within the confines of this colossal cross. But before I give up the ghost, I never answered your question. Was my mother religious? You remember my mentioning the cross positioned over her bed?"

"Of course," Ramey said softly.

"I recall distinctly, when I was but a boy. Walking barefoot down the long hallway on the third floor of our big fancy house. The feeling of the glass knob in my hand as I turned it to open my mother's door. The man standing by her bed with his back to me. Wearing a long-sleeved blue shirt with his trousers lying in a bunch around his black-socked feet. The bare cheeks of his white buttocks clenched tight, dimples along his hairy crevasse. My dear mother peering around the man only to see her son frozen in wide-eyed shock. Her face rosy red, mouth agape, a policeman's cap resting crookedly on her head." Charles sighed. "Religious, you asked? A saint, she was."

"I'm sorry—"

"The man by the bed turned to me," Charles continued. "In my child's curiosity, I glanced at his private part, sticking out, the purplish end bobbing this way and that. Further up, I noticed a star affixed to his loosened shirt. Then the man's incredulous scowl, which caused me to tremble. I could feel my very skin shrinking."

"You shouldn't have had—" Father Ramey began.

"'Charlie!' Mama cried out. 'You *know* the rules,'" Charles continued, seeming to ignore the chaplain's presence altogether. "'Goddamnit,' the man growled. He yanked up his trousers, fastened them, then came toward me, his dark eyes fixed in a hateful glare.

"My mama pleaded, 'Go back up to your playroom, Charlie.' She was trying to cover herself with a sheet. 'Hurry, go on back up,' she said.

"But I did not hurry back to my little attic playroom. I remained in the doorway, frightened as a doe. The police officer proceeded to grab me by the neck of my T-shirt. I instinctively grasped his arm with both hands. He growled at me, 'Listen up, boy. You ain't seen me here. You ain't seen nothin' at all. You understand? You decide to run that little mouth, well...' He glanced back at Mama, then continued in a hushed tone. 'I'll see to it somethin' awful happens to that pretty mama of yours. Ya hear me? Make you an orphan, boy. That sound like somethin' you wanna see happen?'"

Charles went quiet.

Father Ramey shifted in his chair. He crossed his legs as a woman would. "Charles, no child should be brought up in such an environment. But don't let this be an excuse—"

"Here comes the fun part. The watershed, if you will. As I had my little boy hands around the man's sweaty, hairy forearm, a sensation came over me that I could only describe as...ascendancy. I looked that cretin in the eyes and said, 'You have to come here and pay my mama because your wife won't let you touch her.' The words poured from my mouth without deliberation. And somehow, I knew the statement to be an unequivocal fact.

"The back of the officer's hand came hard across my cheekbone. My head spun to the side; saliva flew from my mouth.

"'Please, he's just a young'un,' Mama cried. She shuffled over, wrapped in the sullied sheet, and inserted herself between us. Her back was to me, one arm held out protectively, the other holding the sheet in place. 'He's just a harmless little fool,' she pleaded. 'I'll take him back upstairs, then you can finish up with me. An extra quarter hour, if you want.'

"The cop glared at me from over my mama's shoulder. I could feel my cheek swelling, burning. Yet I was overcome with pride at having delivered such an insult to this towering, contemptible man. It was then my attention moved away from the officer's snarling countenance to the cross above my mama's brass headboard. It had been knocked askew and now hung inverted by a single nail."

Father Ramey remained silent, his expression solemn.

"So, from that time forth," Charles continued glibly, "I've done what poor Charlie couldn't bring his timid little self to do. When our libidinous law enforcement officer reemerged, having us removed from such an 'unfit environment' and delivered to the more wholesome juvenile detention center out in bayou land, I continued to offer my strength to Charlie, remaining in him so that he might endure the myriad impending hardships.

"That's my modus operandi, Father. Why bother with the inherently proud and resilient when the forlorn and down-trodden are an ampler lot? And, more significantly, they yearn for that sweet taste of sovereignty which *your* God has so cruelly withheld from their lips. Sure, Charlie talks rough, but he's spineless...lily-livered. Why, he wouldn't squash a spi-der. Excuse my frankness, but were it not for my influence, he may never have known what it was to truly be a man. Spend-ing his childhood days up there in his private attic room, peeking through the window slats at the world beyond. Only women about to model himself after. Why, how would the boy have ever learned to handle himself in the grueling com-pany of males? He might well have ended up as our new friend Kelly Chase."

Charles took an exaggerated breath and blew it out quickly. He turned to the chaplain and asked, "What do you make of it, Father?"

"The slaughtering of nine people, five of them women,"

Father Ramey said, his mouth scarcely moving. "Is that the action of a true man?"

"Oh my...moving right along, are we? Was my little preamble growing wearisome? Or has the fragrance of my soiled cloth found its way—"

"What is your name?" Ramey snapped. "This current...personality who is speaking."

"Ah...so you *have* rifled my archives, you nosy parker." Charles laughed riotously. He stuck out his tongue, thrashing it obscenely at the chaplain. "Good heavens. A man of the cloth who cannot sniff out the primal stench of iniquity right under his ordained nose?"

Father Ramey's mouth grew taut. Beads of perspiration began to trickle down his brow.

"Charles," Ramey said, with a trace of agitation. "Charles Buck—"

"Oh, stop," Charles said curtly. "I've placed my knee upon his neck, figuratively speaking. It will remain there until it's my will to remove it, Father. And for the record, don't let old Charlie fool you. I offer him glimpses of our past shenanigans as he slumbers. This 'I don't recall' charade is a bit sly on his part."

"Having some awareness doesn't make him responsible for *your* wickedness."

"Fair enough. But it was not *I* who led Charles the eighteen-year-old bearded man back to Basin Street upon his release from the juvenile jail. Although, I must admit a slight pining for the old familiar ambience: the perfumed air, piano music from the parlor, the mischievous giggles... But alas, we discovered the neighborhood of Charlie's childhood had been 'sanitized,' so to speak. Ironically, this *cleansing* left the district a virtual slum. All the madams had either retired or scattered about the city to continue their respective enterprises elsewhere. And Charlie's mother had vanished in the wind.

"Feeling disillusioned, a drunken Charlie took the train from New Orleans and poured himself off at Nashville's Union Station. I remember that wonderfully cool Tennessee evening air. Again, it was Charles who began the quest for female companionship in that fair city. Which we stumbled upon within a Queen Anne in disrepair merely a few blocks away. Though not as grand a facade as that of our Basin Street Victorian, its inner workings proved mutual.

"And I assure you, Father, it was all Charlie in that room. Until...it wasn't. As was often the case with the graceless fool, his ejaculation came in a matter of seconds. When the nice young lady let him know, in no uncertain terms, that his 'turn' was over, I felt his emotions come crashing like waves upon a rocky shore. And when she kicked him off her, literally kicking with her bare feet, dumb Charlie didn't know what to make of it. Thank *God* I was there."

Father Ramey slammed his Bible closed. He leaned forward in his chair and whispered, "Whoever you are, don't ever again thank my righteous Lord for your wickedness."

"Well, don't get testy," Charles said hurtfully. "Anyway...the girl told Charlie that if he wanted another go, he could march his—how was it?—'smelly ass' downstairs and speak to the madam. At this, Charlie grew absolutely indignant."

"Are you saying it was Charles who—"

"Heavens no." A look of resignation came to Charles's face. "Like I said, he had no idea what to do with himself; I had to step in. I twisted the whore's head until she went limp and left her lying like a rag doll on the bed. I pulled on the trousers, the cowboy boots, smoothed Charlie's tousled hair in the vanity mirror, and off we went, from one room to the next..."

"Taking the lives of eight more innocent people with a seven-inch hunting knife," Ramey stated emphatically.

"*Innocent* is a relative term," Charles said. "Oh, how Charlie loved that knife. It had a gorgeous turquoise handle inlaid with colorful stones. He kept it in a sheath fastened to the pull strap of his cowboy boot. The blade was wonderfully engraved—"

"Enough about the knife," Ramey said.

"Oh... Then let's just say, with knife in hand—but enough about the knife—we went about killing both whore and john with equal vigor. Then out the back door we went. Through a muddy yard, over a wood-planked fence, and into a cheap, nearby hotel where Charlie could lay low until it all blew over."

Charles caught Father Ramey staring at the network of scars on his forearm. "Yes, well, days later, Charlie awoke, recalling only bits and pieces. He noticed the bloody shirt tied to his arm. The dead woman in bed next to him. Charlie and whores...what could possibly be his issue?" Charles's body shook with silent laughter. "His feeble mind ran amok with worry. He panicked. The poor fool decided he would end it all right there in that grimy little hotel room.

"Quite the quandary, it was. Me? I was bursting with excitement, teeming with contentment. And this buffoon to whom I've hitched my wagon wants to lead us off a cliff. The selfishness of it! I mean...what about *me*?" Charles sighed. "All dressed up with nowhere to go, as it were.

"I decided old Charlie should stick around, thinking the prison environment might be rather exciting. Like the juvenile jail, but with perhaps even more thrills to be had. And I was quite right. It's been great fun. But, alas, poor Charlie is at his end..."

Charles's chained hand struck out toward Father Ramey. The chaplain shot up from his chair, sending it tumbling backwards onto the concrete floor with a loud clang. He held his Bible against his chest in trembling hands.

"No, no, dear Father," Charles said between chuckles. "Why, you are fully protected by the shed blood of Jesus Christ, Son of the most high God. Indwelt by the Spirit of the Holy Ghost. Number three of the trinity. That stingy old spook who simply refuses to rub shoulders with the likes of me." Charles scoffed. "Goodness no. Filled to the rim, you are. Spilling over even." He ran his long tongue over the wiry hair above his lip while his dark, laughing eyes flitted across the ward, from one row of beds to the other. "Decisions, decisions..."

Father Ramey stepped toward the bed. With a wavering tone, he asked, "Why did you want to see me? Do you feel you've not gotten the attention you deserve? A last posturing before you cease to exist? Or...was it Charles Buckley who requested I see him? And you've such an aversion to him that you would take over simply to deny him a last opportunity at redemption?"

Charles's expression turned contemplative. "None of the above. Charles experienced a moment of weakness. No surprise there. I believe the recent death of an old acquaintance here in the ward served him up a dose of reality. Soon his little conscience was stirred into a tizzy."

"Then why—"

"You and Charles have a shared interest, you might say."

"Stop!" Ramey shouted. The word echoed through the

ward, bringing a medley of responses from the inmate patients.

Charles's eyes widened. "Well, I simply thought we'd compare war stories, but if you're unwilling to reciprocate…"

Father Ramey was now visibly shaking. "I came to Charles out of concern—"

"Perhaps you should be concerned for yourself, dear Father," Charles said. "It must be a tremendous strain upon your wavering soul."

"What do you mean?" Ramey said through clenched teeth.

"Dressed in your holy garb in the brightness of the day," Charles began with lighthearted ambiguity. "Busy with the Lord's work. Then, under the veil of nightfall, off you go to pay a visit to that little place out there, deep in the crevasse of the hills. That rundown clapboard wonderland of flesh that only a privileged few are privy to. Why, I do believe one of your rendezvous was deemed worthy of newsprint."

The chaplain's face turned utterly white. After a long moment, he said, "Mr. Buckley, part of my duties as a man of the cloth is to visit with the lost, just as Jesus—"

"Now *you* stop!" Charles snapped. "I'm done with you, Father."

Ramey turned and scanned the ward, then turned back to Charles. He took a step closer and whispered, "Tell me…if I'm not speaking with Charles Buckley, with whom am I speaking? When I bend my knee in prayer tonight, who shall I tell the Lord is responsible for denying one of his beloved a last opportunity at redemption? Tell me your name."

Charles turned his gaze to the ceiling. He drummed the tips of his fingers on the bed rail and replied, "Puddin' Tame."

Father Ramey offered a bleak smile. "I hope you've

enjoyed your time, sir. Because it's nearing its end." He drew a deep breath, opened his jacket, and tucked the Bible into his pocket.

Charles watched the chaplain walk unhurriedly out the double doors. "I wouldn't be too sure of that, Father."

• • •

Charles awoke to shouts coming from the far end of the ward. Unruly patient Scott Latham was again unleashing a verbal assault upon attendant Kelly Chase. Charles watched with mounting interest.

After a seemingly endless rant, there came a hawking sound followed by *thoo* as Latham spat in Kelly's face. Kelly, embarrassed, quickly wiped the discharge on the sleeve of his shirt, then dutifully finished tending to the patient's wound.

Afterwards, Kelly pushed the table down the middle of the room toward the exit to a chorus of insolent discourse. When he was about to make the turn toward the double doors, Charles called out, "Young Mr. Chase."

Kelly stopped and turned to him.

"Might I have a moment?"

Reluctantly, Kelly left the cart and went to Charles's bedside.

"I wish to apologize for my earlier behavior. When my fever swells, I'm capable of monstrous behavior."

"It's okay. I...thank you," Kelly replied.

"I see you're having quite the time with this domicile of degenerates."

"It's okay," he repeated. "Dr. Swann says they'll ease up after a while."

"It's okay, is it?"

"He says it's just because I'm new."

"Dr. Swann says?"

"He also said he would speak to Mr. Latham for me."

"Plans to give him a good talking to, does he?"

Kelly lowered his head. "Yeah."

"Chin up," Charles said. "The tide will turn."

Kelly smiled and nodded. "I'll be by soon with your nightly doses," he said with a trace of hope in his tenor.

Charles watched Kelly wheel the cart through the double doors.

A good talking to by the doctor? Charles mused. "Let's do better than that, shall we?"

Soon Kelly was back at Charles's bedside. "I have your medications."

"Oh, goody," Charles replied softly.

Kelly set a cup of water on the little table, then raised the container of pills to Charles's mouth.

"I'm sorry, boy," Charles said weakly. "I'm afraid I haven't the strength. You'll need to feed them to me by hand. A pill at a time."

Hesitantly, Kelly picked a large antibiotic tablet from the container and held it up for Charles's approval.

Charles grinned, showing his gapped, nicotine-stained teeth. Then his unusually long tongue jutted from his mouth and began to flicker in a reptilian-like flurry. It retracted just as quickly.

"Sorry," Charles said cheerily. "Down the pipe." He extended his tongue again, keeping it still and letting his lids close slowly over his jaundiced eyes.

Kelly placed the pill atop the elongated organ. Charles clamped down on Kelly's hand, his teeth locking onto bone, his tongue worming around the smooth fingers while he groaned suggestively. Then he released the hold and, smiling, said, "I can take my own medicine, thank you very much." Charles took the container with his thumb and index finger, turned it up, then handed it back.

Kelly's face flushed. He wiped his wet fingers on his pant leg, quickly collected the unused water cup and empty pill container, and pushed his table toward the neighboring bed.

• • •

"I hear you're studyin' up to be a nurse?"

"That's right, I am," Kelly replied, fully aware what course the inquiry would take. "The swelling has gone down."

Scott Latham had been three days in the infirmary with Kelly tending to his nasty knife wound. For three days he had spouted foulmouthed insults, threats of bodily harm, and rude insinuations regarding Kelly's sexual proclivity.

Kelly continued his positive observations. "The redness around the cut has mostly faded—"

"No shit? That's a thing?"

"Sir?" Kelly said, then snickered. "Oh yeah. It's a real thing. There are male nurses. Not many, but it's becoming more common. The states have been slower than some other countries. But men can now be commissioned into the military as nurses. I want to do that one day. My father was in the Army during the second World War."

"You wanna be a *nurse* in the Army? Don't you worry someone'll kick the shit outta ya?"

Kelly smiled passively.

"I mean, you gonna wear the short dress and stockings? And the little white hat?"

Kelly's smile widened as he shook his head dismissively. But the smile quickly faded. His eyes closed. He grimaced, searching blindly for the metal bed rail. Finding it, he held it with a white-knuckled grip.

"Hey, nurse, you need a doctor?" Latham snorted.

"That's just menstrual cramps," someone hollered. "Best fetch you a Midol tablet from the candy closet."

"Nah, she needs a shot of peppermint oil," another suggested. "That always worked for my granny."

"I need to give this one last proper cleaning with peroxide," Kelly said, ignoring the remarks. "Before they release you tomorrow." He let go of the bed rail, then opened and closed his hands.

"Yeah, do it *proper* like, Nurse Kelly."

Kelly turned to his rolling table. He unfolded a towel containing a large syringe. He then emptied the vile of fine white crystals into a cup of water and stirred it with a spoon until it had thoroughly dissolved. He filled the syringe with the milky liquid.

"This could sting a tad, Mr. Latham." Kelly turned to his patient holding the upturned syringe. "But you're a tough one. Judging from your scars, this was hardly your first shanking." He aimed the tip and depressed the plunger rod, causing the liquid to stream into the open wound.

"Aaaww! God*damn* you, mother*fucker*!"

With a contented grin, Kelly covered the paraphernalia with a towel and began his exit to the familiar heckling chorus. Taking his time, he sauntered down the wide aisle between the rows of beds, giving each patient a deliberate smile and a suggestive wink as Latham howled in agony.

Just before turning toward the double doors, Kelly glanced at his newest patient, who lay in the bed in which

Charles Buckley had recently succumbed. "Mr. Messing…" He paused with one hand on the table's handlebar, the other on his hip. "Have I told you what a blessing you are to me? Mr. Buckley"—Kelly raised his head to the ceiling—"rest in peace. He could be such a grumpy bear at times."

Messing slowly shook his head.

"Anyway, I'll be back with your meds in two shakes." Kelly grinned and thrust his hip to the left, then the right.

"You can stick them meds where the sun don't shine, Nurse Kelly," came Messing's reply.

"Oh, my!" Kelly cried out. He cupped a hand over his rear end, then pranced on through the double doors, humming cheerily.

He pushed the cart into the medicine closet. Its shelves were lined with bottles of pharmaceuticals, bandages, and other medical necessities. On the floor sat jugs of industrial cleaning products along with boxes of rat poison for use on those mangy scoundrels that occasionally found their way into the infirmary.

•••

By the turn of the millennium, the so-called "Sandstone Cross" was well past its centennial and its applicability. In the years following its closing, it fell into disrepair, hosting the occasional Halloween scare fest and myriad vermin. Eventually, the property was purchased by a group of entrepreneurs who repurposed the castle-like compound into an unlikely tourist attraction. Subsequently, those filing through the "gates of hell" can enjoy a good sit-down meal at the Bean

Slot Tavern, and purchase a variety of branded apparel, trinkets, or souvenir moonshine from the Commissary Gift Shop. A small museum displays a trove of physical artifacts while its walls are lined with plaques chronicling the prison's history. Perhaps the most popular activity are the daily tours of the prison grounds and cell block buildings led by former inmates or guards, whose personal recollections lend authenticity to their narratives.

This had been the snippet the man recently found on a website after he'd submitted a search. The tour sounded fascinating, but after the long and somewhat inclined trek from the parking lot, he'd decided against it. His recently replaced knee had been taxed enough.

He'd enjoyed a pulled-pork sandwich platter and purchased a coffee mug in the gift shop. Presently, he sat on a bench positioned along the wall of the museum, which held a dozen or so informational plaques mentioned on the website's promotional blurb.

The two teenage boys swaggered up to the plaque next to where he sat. "The Infirmary Murders," the smaller of the two read aloud.

"Oh, look. Nurse Kelly is a dude," the arrogant one said.

"He looks gay," said the other.

"You would know," the bigger one said, giving his companion a hard slap on the back.

"Ow," the smaller one cried.

"Ooowww," the other whined mockingly. "Keep moving," he said, shoving the other ahead of him.

The man watched them as they moved to the next plaque.

The arrogant one, following behind, swiped the legs of his buddy, causing him to fall forward onto his knees. Several visitors turned their way as the boy quickly got to his feet, his face red with embarrassment.

Nurse Kelly, the man repeated in his mind. He got to his feet, groaning, and went to the plaque where the two boys had departed. He studied the two grainy sepia photographs within its composition. One candid shot snapped by a news photographer showed a handcuffed subject being escorted by arresting officers into the Davidson County Corrections building in Nashville. The other was of the Sandstone Cross's hospital staff lined up along the carved-stone exterior wall, a sign on the door to their left indicating "INFIRMARY." The man scanned the faces and caption, then read the synopsis in full.

> From February 1952 until September 1953, Mr. Kelly Chase (better known by the derogative "Nurse Kelly") worked part time as a ward attendant in the prison's infirmary while studying for a degree in nursing. During Chase's brief tenure at the prison hospital, eight inmates died, none designated terminal. Under mounting suspicion, Chase vacated his position without notice. He was arrested twenty-one days later in Nashville after a man called the police to report a break-in at his downtown residence. He further revealed that the strange man was currently asleep in his daughter's bed. When the police arrived, Mr. Chase appeared bewildered, unable to tell the responding officers what had brought him to that particular home, the site where multiple slayings

had occurred years earlier when it served as a house of prostitution. He was arrested for breaking and entering, but under further interrogation, Mr. Chase made mention his possible wrongdoings at a prison infirmary. After a thorough psychiatric evaluation deemed him fit to stand trial, he was found guilty of causing the deaths of eight patients while working at the infirmary here at the Sandstone Cross. Methods included poisoning, intentional pharmaceutical overdose, as well as a singular admission to manual asphyxia. His life sentence was served elsewhere as the judge deemed incarceration within the institution at which he'd committed his crimes to be "unnecessarily prejudicial." "Nurse" Kelly Chase died of natural causes in August of 1977 at the Cumberland Correctional Facility's hospital.

The man suddenly grew dizzy. He leaned forward, placing his palms on either side of the plaque to keep himself upright. He closed his eyes as tremors rippled through his body. His mind raced with visions of naked prostitutes and their johns clambering about in disheveled beds. A brass bedframe. An inverted cross swaying on a wall. A turquois-handled knife. Blood-splattered faces fixed in horrified death masks. A water-stained ceiling. Squeaking wheels along a concrete floor. Agonizing moans from the dreadful inmate-patient Scott Latham as strychnine infused his oozing gash. The feeling of utter helplessness as the judge's bald threats toward him echoed within the locked door of his otherwise empty chambers. The overwhelming sensation as Kelly Chase embraced him after being illicitly deemed competent to stand trial based on the court's appointed psychiatric professional's coerced conclusions. And lastly, he saw in distinct detail the bloated, panicked visage of dishonorable Judge Harold Dreyfus as the constricting wire collapsed his windpipe.

When the old man opened his eyes, his own terrified reflection stared back at him from the plexiglass casing. He could hear the teenage boys snorting and guffawing. He lifted his hands off the wall and steadied himself. He combed the bangs off his forehead with his fingers. He blinked his eyes and drew several calming breaths.

When he turned to face the boys, they attempted to hide their amusement. The man granted a smile and a nod for their effort. Then he wrapped a knuckle on the plexiglass and said aloud, "Oh my. Now this young fellow here, he was most fascinating."

The cocky one snickered under his breath. The smaller shushed him.

Unperturbed, the man continued his commentary. "I was the psychiatrist tasked with gauging Mr. Chase's mental capacity to stand trial for these so-called infirmary murders. I didn't realize until sometime later that the poor lad could no more stifle his violent impulses than a fighting dog could release its opponent's throat from the grasp of its jaws. 'Dissociative identity disorder' they call it these days—DID. A tricky concept, I must say."

The boys shared quizzical glances.

Having gained their full attention, the man continued. "Oh, how the decades swiftly lapse. I rather enjoy revisiting venues from my past. Especially those I feel I've...left my mark upon."

"Oookay, dude," the tough one replied with a roll of his eyes.

"Dude? Oh, please..." the man countered, offering his hand. "We can do better than that."

With a smirk fixed on his acned face, the kid slapped the man's open palm. As he pulled his hand away, the man took his wrist in a viselike grip. "The name is Osman. And yours, you deplorable crotchling?"

"Aaagh," the boy groaned, his face twisting in pain. "Bri...an," he managed to answer.

The man released him, then turned to his underling with his hand still extended. "And you, young man?"

"Tommy," the boy replied, avoiding eye contact.

"And this killer with you? He's your friend?"

"He's my brother."

When the boy tried to pull his hand away, the man tightened his grip. "Oh... Well, that explains it," he said knowingly. "You can't very well escape the tyrannous realm of big brother now, can you?"

The boy made an awkward attempt at a smile.

"Tell me, is he *ever* kind to you?"

"Let him go, you wrinkled old fuck," big brother spat.

"Let him go?" the man repeated mockingly. He firmly enveloped the smaller boy's hand in both of his own. "Oh... I don't think I will. Not for a good, long while."